C. James Kelly

Thunder Well

© 2013, C. James Kelly

Some Reading Required Co.

All characters appearing in this work are fictitious. Any resemblance to real persons, living or dead, is purely coincidental.

THUNDER WELL

This book is dedicated to my wife Vicki
for always inspiring me and encouraging me
to be the best that I can be.

THUNDER WELL

There was a crispness in the air, here above the tree line. It smacked of fall and an early winter. If there had been broad leaf trees this high up they would have turned color and started to shed their summer wares. Still, you could smell the dampness that came with the on-set of fall. As it was you could see your breath and if you inhaled sharply enough you could stick your nostrils together. Snow had come to the peaks and it wouldn't be long before Simons perch would be to icy to be safe.

As he headed back to the ten inch thick steel door that was carved into the cliff face behind him, Simon reflected on a day forty years earlier where in this same spot, he had set off an explosion that in its time seemed horrifying in its intensity but now would only be the catalyst to set something in motion insane in intention and mankind's last hope for redemption.

It was May in Nevada, 1957. The nights were still cool but the days were warm and sunny. Simon and his team had been using fission or thermonuclear and plasma waves with a sunken shaft configuration to try to propel objects into space.

They had come by the idea quite by accident when on a previous test a heavy metal cap that secured the shaft went missing after the ensuing nuclear blast and was never found.

Some theorized that it was vaporized by the heat generated from the explosion but others believed that it had been launched to the moon.

Either way, at the ripe old age of 23, Simon was having a great old time blowing shit up in the Nevada desert with the biggest explosives still not known to man.

The crazy thing was he actually thought it might work. Some of the earlier shafts had some design flaws that kept the projectiles from making it out of their sunken dens but they had come up with a way to grade the shaft and actually rifle the sides so that upon detonation the plasma wave itself actually spun as it drove its projectile to the surface. That had solved getting the object to escape velocity but the rifling at that speed made the object spin at such a velocity that there would be no way anything could carry a payload into orbit without it being entirely liquefied as if it were in a blender.

It had taken six months of all-nighters to come up with what Simon and his team thought was a viable work around for the spin problem and they had scheduled a date to test their theory. They had even gone so far as to have carved a new shaft with the specific dimensions worked into its walls. A secluded place, high in the Rocky Mountains a good day's drive from Cheyenne Wyoming. A new devise had been commissioned and they were awaiting its arrival. What arrived was a cease and desist order from his superiors.

For weeks they had heard rumors that the bleeding heat liberals up in Washington had been holding closed door hearings on the effect of so many atomic detonations on the environment and what effect the fallout might have on animal and human populations in these test site areas. Simon had heard the talk but he had always been too involved in the science to wonder what the consequences of the experiments he and his fellow colleagues were performing had on his surroundings.

Now they had been shut down without as much as a heads up or a where too next.

After that Simon stumbled around from job to job, always with the science community and always on Government projects. Some he liked some he didn't. It mattered little to him. No matter how hard he worked or how hard he played he never really got over his pet project, trying to blow things into space.

1998

The Paddy Wagon wasn't much of a bar, at least not in its present condition. In its day it had seen some of Detroit's finest through its doors. It took its name because it resided two doors down from the 12th precinct on Beaubien and had long been the watering hole for justice and thug alike.

Nowadays it was a mere shell of its once opulent self. The framed images of heroic officers gone by had seen one too many bar fights. Broken and toppled they lay on one another in ever growing dust that was the only cushion to keep them from being completely destroyed. The pool table, bottle stained and worn, had a distinct list to one end as it followed the sagging floor boards on their inevitable way to the cellar below. The bar had heard many a tale of crime and punishment to the point where it could hear no more and it had become only a landing strip for fruit flies as it lay waiting for someone to put it out of its misery.

Simon loved the place. He could still remember it in its hay day. Men and women in blue celebrating a great bust or morning a fellow officer downed in the line of duty. The old owner, Carlos, a Cuban guy with a great laugh was always willing to spot a fellow a couple of drinks between pay checks. The place was cool in the summer and warm in the winter and nobody messed with you no matter how drunk you got because everyone was a regular and everyone was family.

Carlos had disappeared in Feb 1961. Disappeared in that he had sold the place and left without much explanation. It was rumored that he had gone with fellow exiles to free his beloved Cuba and was never heard from again after the Bay of Pigs. The new owner was never seen in the place and it soon fell into disrepair. Bar tenders came and went along with a litany of good looking but sleazy waitresses. No matter, this was Simons place. Three or four times a week he could be found sitting in the corner nursing a bourbon and branch. Waiting for some old patron to fall through the door and reminisce. He sometimes thought even a stick up would be something different but no one ever robbed the place and old faces seldom made an appearance.

Summer hadn't turned yet but the shadows were getting longer and the sun was heading south. Fall was coming quick to Detroit and soon the 1998 Detroit Redwings would be rolling out this seasons new batch of bruisers and brawlers in another attempt at hockey's Holy Grail, the Stanley Cup. It was Tuesday night and Simon was in his usual place at the Paddy. Not really expecting anything to change but always more hopeful with a couple of bourbons under his belt. The door opened and a damp wind blew in from the street. It brought an odor of rotting leaves and wet dog hair that made Simon glance up from his perusal of the table top.

The man in the door way didn't fit the usual look of the Paddy Wagon clientele. His trench coat smacked of money and the suit, visible through the unbuttoned front, was free of the sheen that comes with wearing the same clothes day after day.

This, thought Simon, would be something more interesting than trying to figure out what was sticking to his feet under the table he was at.

The door closed and as Simon stared the man in the coat stared back and began walking toward him.

Now Simon was never one to start things up. He preferred to be on the periphery whenever a dust up occurred in the bar. That wasn't to say that he didn't enjoy a good donnybrook every now and again. Just to break up the monotony you understand. But he always made sure he was out of the way with his back to the wall so if nothing else, he wouldn't spill his drink and he could get a good seat for the fight.

That being said Simon knew intent when he saw it and this guy was focused on him. Did he know him? The guy was too young to be any one he knew.

Had the guy mistaken him for someone else? Hopefully not someone who owed money. That was never good.

Simon had a few years under his belt but he was no slouch. Even after being pulled from the Thunder Well project he kept up with a steady regimen. Three days at the gym and two times a week he got in a five or ten kilometer run in. The routine had kept his six foot frame well-muscled and his cardio pretty decent. Still would he be able to handle this guy if he started something up?

Too many questions and not enough floor space. The newcomer was at his table and making moves to sit down.

"Simon Forman?" The guy was evidently looking for him.

Simon just nodded.

"I thought you would be a lot harder to track down." Hmmm, a wise guy, Simon thought.

"Hey, don't look so scared, I'm here to ask you for help"

"I'm not scared." Simon retorted. "It's just you're the first sober person to come through the door in a week." He could be a wise guy too.

"Ok, good." The guy said looking about with a bit of trepidation himself. He was probably just realizing what a dive he had wondered into.

"Now who's scared?" Simon asked.

Simon didn't think the guy was scared one bit. As he had passed through the doorway Simon noticed that the top of his head wasn't very far under the frame and if it had been any smaller in width the guy would have got stuck on the way in.

"I have a business proposal for you from your country."

Great, Simon thought, another shit job from the boys in white shirts at the office.

As Simon had aged he had passed on the usual promotions in the branch. His work for the government was basically science but his idea of research wasn't sitting behind a desk six days a week using a slide rule to try and figure out how big his ass was getting. He loved the lab or the field. It didn't matter which and he was content with the money he made. Bosses came and went, getting younger as the years went by and as those years passed the outside work became less and less likely. Computer testing was the way now but Simon found that without the big boom and the ground shaking under foot, it just didn't have the same good feeling about it. The fun had gone out of it and as it was Simon could probably grab another afternoon at the Paddy if he so desired.

"We already know that you work for the government and we know you're not too happy, haven't been for years. We also know about the work you did back in the day so what you say we go somewhere with a bit more shine on it so I can give you our proposal in a friendlier environment."

"First of all, who's we?" Simon asked. "And there is nowhere around here that's any shinier or friendlier than this."

Simon's new friend reached into his jacket and brought out a zippered document case. He pulled a small sheaf of papers out and handed them to Simon. They were yellowed with age and looked well read.

Simon instantly recognized the letter head. These were notes Simon had submitted in the 50's while he was developing his fission and plasma theories and blowing shit up. This stuff was top secret. Where had this lump gotten his hands on secret government archives?

The next item out of the coat was a small leather bound wallet that opened to revealed trench coats identification and though Simon had not seen hi level security docs in some time he recognized the real thing when they were presented.

Funny, in his brief glance at the passport, he noticed the guy's name was Nick. Somehow he thought it was going to be Russian or something. Mind you, Nick could be short for Nikolai.

"Ok, you got my attention. What do you want?"

The guy stood up. Yup, he is a big boy, Simon thought.

"Look, we need your help but let's get somewhere besides this to talk"

Nick was about to tell the guy you couldn't get much friendlier than the Paddy but he had heard just the slightest hint of desperation in the new comers' voice and figured what the hell, I can't get much more bored or feel less useless than sitting in this place. Besides the guys documents were legit

"I got no car, so you'll have to drive."

"I'm right out front." The stranger said.

"I got no money, so you'll have to buy."

"I got money."

Simon stood and followed out the door. Didn't even look back to see if Jimmy the bartender noticed he didn't pay his bill.

Screw it; I put enough money into this place over the years I could have bought it and turned it into a dump myself.

The hummer was indeed out front. Government plates to boot. The anomaly was the color. Baby blue.

"Shit, if this is supposed to be inconspicuous, it ain't working." Simon said under his breath.

"I hear ya man." Trench coat piped up. "It was the only thing in the pool when they sent me out to find you."

Guy must have the hearing of an owl, Simon thought to himself this time.

Simon jumped up into the passenger seat. One look told him things had changed since the last time he had been in a new vehicle. This thing was insane.

Nick started the engine with a button. Simon heard it turn over but then there was utter silence in the cab. He couldn't even feel a vibration through the floor. A soft blue light emanated from the control panel in front of the steering wheel that lit up a litany of moving graphs and digital numbers but what really drew Simon's attentions was the sharp green glow that was apparently imbedded in the windshield.

"What the hell is that?" Simon pointed to the middle of the windshield.

"That, my friend, is the heads up display. A great little tool if you don't want to look down to see how fast you're going."

Nick looked pretty happy about that piece of technology and Simon was thinking to himself, where the hell have I been that this has been going on and I have missed it.

Simon had never been one to be reflective and he wasn't going to start now but he did in this moment have one small pang of regret. He thought of the years he had wasted sitting in a memory. Why had he not pursued some avenue of experiment that suited his skill set? Instead of mopping about for years wishing for his old job back?

All that time he could have been productive. He had always known, deep down the there was a hidden underbelly in the government building. People working away on hidden projects. He would have fit right in.

Nick had pulled the Hummer into traffic and was headed east. The sky had turned a color gray that suggested rain.

Simon figured it didn't matter what the weather, this vehicle was made to handle it.

The Hummer dodged in and out of the building rush hour traffic like a car half its size. Simon thought, if nothing else, this guy is a pretty good driver.

"So Nick, you gonna tell me where we're going. I mean, I live in the neighborhood so you're gonna give me a ride back right?"

Nick looked over with a stupid grin on his face.

"Depends on what you think of our little proposal."

"Well, spill." Simon pushed. "What is this, some kinda black and white fifties spy movie shit."

"Ok, look, I know a place about ten minutes away where we're a little less likely to get shot while we have a drink. I'll give you the set up on the way."

Nick turned right on Woodward and headed toward the Detroit Medical Centre.

"So here's the skinny." Nick began. "It really started in 1977. You heard of the wow signal I assume?"

"Ya." Nick snorted. Hopefully with enough sarcasm that Nick realized he was just disillusioned with his job not stupid.

"Right." Nick glance over. "Sorry. You probably know more about it than me. Anyway, it has always been reported that the signal had come from somewhere in the constellation Sagittarius likely near the Chi Sagittarii star group."

Simon was nodding. This was stuff he had researched himself when the wow signal had been reported in 77.

"Well what no one knows is that is exactly where it came from, the signal that is."

Simons surprise must have been evident because Nick didn't even give him a second to reflect on that piece of news before really dropping the bomb.

"But that's not the scary part of it. Remember all the controversy on what the signal might mean and even though they had some of the best minds in the country and around the world testing, no one could figure out if the signal meant anything?"

Simon just nodded. Not really even hearing Nick speak, his mind wheeling around trying to grasp the idea that they actually knew it was real. That there really was a signal and therefore someone must have sent it and therefore some other form of intelligent life. "Holly Shit!" Simon barely squeaked.

"Ya, well here is the shit man; they did find out what the message was. It wasn't all that complicated. It pretty much said. We know you're out there and we're coming to get you." I'm paraphrasing here but they didn't mean it in a nice way."

Simon felt like he was in some kind of trance. It was actually the sound of his own heart pounding in his ears that brought him back to the inside of the Hummer now pulling over in front of the Hockey Town Café. It was nuts. This guy had just told him that there really were aliens and they were just going to walk into a local sports bar and talk about it while they sipped beers and stole glances at the pub TV's blaring out the pre-season hockey game of the week.

Simon finally found his voice. "You're shittin me right?"

It was more rhetorical than anything.

"I shit you not."

And Simon could tell by the look on the big man's face, he really wasn't shittin.

The place was, as Simon had suspected full of hockey fans, mostly young medical types some still in there greens from the center down the street. They pushed their way through the mêlée at the bar; a couple of the boy's slamming tequila shooters trying to get into the lame pre-season, no hitting game that was spread across five big screens behind the over worked bar keep. They were all the way to the back of the building before they found a small seat for two far enough away from the blaring sets to talk without screaming at each other.

When they had ordered Simon spoke first. "This is crazy. How could they keep this from the American people for so long? You would think that someone, something would have leaked." Nick just shrugged.

Even though Simon truly thought the idea of their actually being another race of beings out there in the Universe, was pretty cool. He quickly realized that all the alien conspiracy theorists had been right. Roswell, the whole thing. Shit, Shit, Shit. And what the hell did the government have up its sleeve that could possibly involve him?

Nick had taken a pretty good swig of his beer before he spoke again. But when he did it left Simon thinking he was going to need something a whole lot stronger than beer to cope with what he had been told.

"So I guess you're wondering what your part in this craziness is, right?" Simon just waited. "So, like I told you in the car. They knew what the message was back in 77. They knew it but they couldn't let the public know that not only did aliens exist but they had a hate on for us for some reason. That would have sent the entire planet into a global freak out.

Can you imagine the panic? How could you tell everyone that they really had no place to go? Unless you had your own space ship you were stuck. Man, what a joke."

Nick just shook his head.

"They didn't give me the details of the message but they made it pretty clear that our new found friends are coming and they ain't coming in peace."

Nick took a deep breath. "So here's the skinny. The project came down to a new government agency. The SDI (Strategic Defense Initiative).

That almost made beer come out of Simon's nose. He had heard of the project and had lobbied long and hard to get in on it.

The project had been initiated by President Ronald Reagan in 1983. The object was to use ground and space-based systems to develop a strategic laser and nuclear ballistic missile system.

Nick didn't notice Simon's laps in attention. "The Commissions task was simple. Find a way to protect earth. Not against our neighbors the Russians or the Chinese like you saw in the news every day, but against whoever showed up from up there."

Nick pointed a big round finger skyward. "You're part you ask? There were billions allocated to the SDI project and there was billions spent but you know what? Not one of the systems developed by these dicks ever worked. If you ask me, too much time spent jacking around with nifty toys and technology and not enough time spent on a practical defense strategy.

I think they thought the ones who sent the wow signal would never come at least not in their lifetimes. Well their coming and all the big ideas are just a bit too little too late.

So here's where you come in. Remember back in the fifties you worked on a project to send a projectile into space using plasma bursts in underground silos? It got shut down just when you claimed you had made the break through to get the job done right? Well get your thinking cap back on buddy boy cause their re-instating the program."

Simon thought he was going to throw up. Had he heard right? It was just too much all at once. Aliens, his pet project back on the table. His head was spinning and he had to put both elbows on the table to keep from falling right off his chair.

Nick took Simons silence to continue his proposal. "So, you would be working under the title of SDI but you would have full control over anyone who worked on the project. You would be given full access to your old files and locations as well as security clearance for any updates in technology that you think you might be able to make use of. That includes nukes, plasma or whatever you needed to further the plan.

"This is no joke. This whole thing is considered DEFCON 1 priority"

"But that level has never been used before." Simon's throat was so dry he barley squawked the words out.

"That's how seriously the boys at the Pentagon are taking this. They have figured out a time frame for contact and it's closer than is comfortable. The President wants some functional line of defense and he wants it now. They have exhausted most of the usual recourses and now you're up. I hope you can supply whatever it is you used to do because I think otherwise we are in for a real shit show."

Simon was stunned. It had been so many years that he had truly given up hope of ever reviving his old project.

In the beginning he had cried long and hard and talked to anyone who would listen. He and his team had made the break through that would allow them to blast objects into space using silo shaped wells with plasma ignition that kept the payload intact. That meant that anything could be launched to escape velocity without the fear of damaging whatever was on board including animal or even human matter. The other possibility was that it would not matter the size of the load. The force of the plasma ignition could be controlled by the length and the rifling of the tube the projectile was launched from and the size of the plasma load. Such simple technology with such a great impact and inexpensive compared to firing solid fuel based vehicles into space.

He had called it project Thunder Well but his lobbying fell on deft ears. Budget cuts were in line and those in the right places were more impressed with the shiny bells and whistle of new technology than digging holes and setting of explosions. And who could blame them. At the time his project involved old and scary techniques of the Cold War area. On one hand you had beautiful looking space craft being hoisted into space with loud powerful rockets, taking man to the moon and beyond. On the other, creating atomic reactions at the bottom of a man made well to force objects into the sky. It was easy to see how one could be tricked into thinking one was different from the other.

The sounds and smells of the bar came back into focus as the reality of what he had just been told sank in. The volume on the hockey game being played above their heads rose to a new level as the Red Wings scored their third goal in the first period. As his vision cleared Simon could see that his revelation and request for help was as insignificant as asking for a bagel and coffee for breakfast at the Starbucks for his new friend Nick who was sitting halfcocked in his seat craning his neck toward one of the big screens hanging from the ceiling.

"Looks like the Wings might win one this year." Nick had more than enough sarcasm in his voice to get his point across.

Still, Simon was amazed at the nonchalance. How could this guy be so unconcerned?

"You don't seem too concerned about any of this Nick." Simon suggested.

That brought Nicks focus back to the table.

"I've been living with this for quite some time Simon."

Nick suddenly looked exhausted. His broad shoulders slumped and he hung his head as he continued.

"For four years I have been on this project in one form or another. I came to it right out of University. I wanted to be a geneticist. You know? Discover the gnome that would save the world? I even graduated from the School of Biological Sciences at the University of Texas with a Master's Degree in Genetics and Microbiology. I was recruited in my last year by the SDI. What I was told at the time was that I would be assisting in development of a non-human invasive organism that could potentially incapacitate any alien life form. The object of the project was to somehow pollute an area of atmosphere somewhere between outer space and our own breathable shield. The layer would be invisible to any alien enemy but would contain microscopic nanites that could penetrate and contaminate anything they came in contact with no matter how air tight. These nanites would potentially carry some muscle or tissue invader that once they gained access to a threat, would release into the atmosphere. Even if the initial layer cloud didn't penetrate a vehicle the nanites would attach themselves to whatever they came in contact with and at some point there would have to be a hatch opened or a probe sent out. That would be when the nanites would get to an enemy before they entered our atmosphere. Basically poison outer space. The theory was that any living thing that could travel to our world would have to breathe somehow. If we created a corona around our own atmosphere with a poisonous layer of disease carrying nanites they would eventually have to ingest some of it and would be incapacitated.

My job was to develop some new strain of hungry microbe that would attack anything it came into contact with that wasn't of our world and find a way to make it symbiotic with the nanites."

Nick could see the look he was getting from Simon.

"I know what you're thinking. The muscles got a brain? Not likely. They send me out on these jobs because I look the way I do. It helps to get the offer across when the person of interest is a bit intimidated. It also helps that I spent my summers selling cars on my uncle's car lot back in New Jersey when I was in school. If you can sell used cars in Jersey you can sell anything so they usually send me out for these little white collar chats.

Simon was beginning to believe that he had somehow fallen asleep back at the Paddy and had woke up in the middle of some crazy spy novel. It just couldn't be real.

Aliens, government cover ups, crazy talk of nanites and macrobiotic technology and a car salesman from Jersey who claimed to be a biologist for a top secret group trying to save the world. If he wasn't going nuts this was going to be one hell of an adventure.

Nick dropped Simon off at his home three blocks from the Paddy Wagon. As he jumped down from the Hummer Nick talked out the open door.

"We really need help here Simon. Please think about coming on board and helping us get something viable into the air. I know I for one could use a regular guy around the place. Just to have someone to talk to that could understand a point spread or talk hockey for a couple of minutes.

"How will I get in touch with you?" Simon asked.

"I'll give you the week and drop back into the Paddy same time next week. It will give me an excuse to get out and have a beer if nothing else."

Simon just nodded as he turned to his street.

HOME TIME

The neighborhood had degenerated over the years but was still a reasonably safe place to live. The fact that the Police station was not far away and the block consisted mostly of the original owners who still took great pride in their homes had something to do with it. While Detroit withered around them Simon's hood remained in good shape.

The trees had all matured in the years since they were planted and they had never had to cut any down to make way for progress. The big oak on Dan Millar's front yard had been struck by lightning five years ago and the city had condemned it. Dan had hired a bunch of guys he knew to come out and clean it up but they had only cleared the broken limbs that were in danger of hitting the roof or the power lines out front. The city never came back to see if he had taken it down and in a few years it had pretty much grown back to its original splendor.

They had started their block association in the early 70's. Their mandate was nothing more than to maintain and help their neighbors and the neighborhood. Through the years some had come and gone but most of the original home owners were still on the street and still with the association. They did monthly bottle walks; they called them, to clean up any old bottles and debris that was left lying about. If a neighbor was away for a period of time they would take turns checking the house and cutting the lawn so it would appear that someone was still around. If one of the elder home owners needed help with painting or cleaning a group would be organized to help out. And if there was any trouble the committee was quick to hire off duty police to make sure that gangs and punks found their street a not so good place for them to be. All in all it was as quiet as it was going to get in these times.

Simon pushed open the arched front door. There were four square lead glass windows in the top and an old styled peep hole in it that was really just a hole drilled about head high right through it. A swinging metal plate covered it and could be moved side to side if anyone came knocking. Simon had found it lying in a pile of broken furniture and drywall pieces at the dump. Obviously someone was renovating and had thrown it out. He still saw the beauty in it. So he brought it home and had an old friend arch the dormer in the front to accommodate it. Now it was the center piece of his home.

Simon flipped on the lights and flung himself down in the arm chair that faced his TV. This was where he spent many nights after the drudgery of work and after a few at the paddy, it was all he could do to even watch the news and feign interest. Most would have thought he lived frugally. The typical older bachelor slash scientist. Books piled willy nilly, take out boxes stacked in the sink and frayed edges on the well-loved furniture. Not so. Simon had loathed how the interior of his home was looking old and used so five years ago he had gone into the city and hired a good designer to renovate the entire top two floors.

What came out after six months of living in a hotel and about one hundred and eighty thousand dollars was an upscale look that almost came off like an expensive Vegas hotel. Lots of marble counter space and huge bathrooms on both floors. The kitchen was gourmet and had all the conveniences even a gas stove. Not that Simon spent a lot of time in the kitchen. He couldn't even remember the last time he had anyone over for a meal and a glass of wine but he did like to stop at the store on the way home most nights and pick up something fresh for dinner.

He had tried stocking up. At least that's what all his neighbors had encouraged him to do.

"You'll save a ton of money if you buy in bulk." They told him.

It didn't take to long for Simon to realize that the bulk went quickly bad around his place. He couldn't eat it fast enough once it had thawed out or if he bought fruit or vegetables by the bag, they rotted before he would get around to slicing and dicing.

No he liked to stop and chat with the people who owned the market where he shopped and he didn't mind having just enough around the house to get by. No one ever dropped in and the neighbors never came by to borrow a cup of sugar or milk so he just lived day to day and that was good enough for him.

He flipped on the TV but it was just noise. His brain was going a mile a minute. Did the last couple of hours just happen or was it some kind of brain cramp that had left him delusional and in shock? Maybe someone had slipped him a little LSD into his drink at the Paddy.

That was a ludicrous though. He hadn't heard anyone using LSD since the sixties.

The only explanation was that it must be legit. That Nick was a real person and everything he had said was true no matter how absurd it sounded. It was sounding more and more absurd sitting here in the comfort of his living room.

Simon couldn't begin to put it all into perspective. He chased the few drinks he had had earlier with a couple of stiff bourbons from the bottle of Jack Daniels he kept over the fridge and was soon snoring like an overweight sideshow fat man with a deviated septum.

THIS WEEK

Simon woke the day after his astonishing night with Nick, the not so nerdy agent for the SDI, still in his cloths from the night before. He was slouched down in his favorite chair with the TV blaring. He could still taste the Jack when he burped and he knew if he did that to many times it would make him sick to his stomach.

Simon liked bourbon but he could not afford the good stuff all the time. The Jack Daniels was a poor man's bourbon and it did the trick in a pinch but the after effects? Sometimes he thought it wasn't worth the day with stomach cramps and fuzzy head.

The week went by slowly. After his adventure with Nick, Simon had rolled a whole bunch of what ifs around in his head but as day three came and went he had started to think that maybe some of the guys at the office were playing some elaborate joke on him. At the end of day four he had actually pushed the whole thing aside as a prank, even though no one at work had laid claim to the fact.

Simon had ended the weekend helping out next door. The Johansen's were getting up there and according to Milly, that was the old girls name, her husband Stan had just not been able to find the time to get the leaves cleaned up and out to the curb.

Simon was pretty sure that both of them had forgotten and had only just come outside to pick up the stack of newspaper and flyers that were accumulating on the porch, when in a timely lucid moment realized that the leaves were piled just as high.

So Simon had volunteered to rake. He would later tell Dan Millar that the two weren't as out of it as they let on and that he was pretty sure they had played on his good nature to get their front yard cleaned up.

Tuesday came and it had been a week since Simon had met with Nick. As he sat at his usual place, backed into a corner at the Paddy, he didn't even give the encounter a second thought. That is until the door opened and Nick came waking in big as ever with the same look of purpose on his face.

Simon would have sworn on a stack of bibles, if anyone had asked that the whole thing was a dream. Brought on by that crappy Jack Daniels he had drank the week before. But Jack or no Jack his dream buddy Nick planted himself down beside Simon and ordered a beer.

"Jeeze, Simon, you look like you just saw your mom in her undies." Nick said.

Well, ha ha, Simon thought, I have seen my mom in her undies but what he didn't want to admit was that Nick scared him a whole lot more than his mom. As a matter of fact, last week he had listened in awe at the story he had been told and he had thought, how remarkable it would be if even half of it were true. Since then he had kind of blown it off as some half-baked dream or DDT from a bad batch of booze and not enough sleep. The reality of seeing Nick back in the bar and sitting next to him was pretty scary.

"So, you going to join us? Come and save the world? I looked you up. You made some pretty big noise back in the day. I think you're just what we need down at the bunker. A little old school shit. Common man, I need a grounding point. I'm so sick of all the techies that I could just puke. What do ya say? Look, we need something you got. This is real and you can't turn you back on your country, right? Besides, this is your chance to get back in the game. It didn't look like you wanted to give up in the first place so now this is your chance to come back. Show those guys in the big office that you knew what you were doing the first time. No questions asked."

That had been one hell of a tirade Simon thought. He really hadn't heard any of it. He was still trying to process the fact that the guy had actually come back and was offering him his old gig back.

"Honestly, I didn't think you were real let alone serious. I had convinced myself that it was some kind of hallucination."

Simon could see Nick staring at him. He had a look like, what the fuck man?

"Well, I'm real and I'm telling you that say yes and you will start tomorrow, at a significant pay raise I might add. So even if the whole world goes to shit in a handbag in the near future you will at least have some money to enjoy it."

Simon gave his head a shake. This was it. The thing that had been gnawing at him for years tossed right in his lap. So why was he hesitating? Ya, fuck it, he said to himself. Nothing ventured, nothing gained.

"Ok, how, where and when." Simon wasn't going to waste another second wondering how this would all come out. He was jumping in feet first.

"Great, this is going to be great." Nick looked pretty happy and when he slapped Simon on the back his enthusiasm was almost as real as the welt the impact of his hand was going to leave.

Nick ordered another couple of drinks and they sat for an hour, hunched over the table like two conspirators in some 1950's Bogart spy movie, while Simon got the basic details of the job. If the information Nick provided was true this was going to be like the old days only better. It sounded pretty much like there was no ceiling on expenses. Get the job done no matter the cost, was what Nick had said.

Nick left as the Paddy began to fill with its usual Tuesday night patrons. He had made arrangements to pick up Simon in the morning so he could take him to the office, where ever that was, and get him introduced and squared away. Simon sat for a while almost in a daze. He really felt like a couple more good strong belts but he talked himself out of it. Tomorrow would be the start of a new day for him. Even if it was the beginning of the end after all, he thought, maybe I'll give this thing a real good try and show those ass holes that THUNDER WELL wasn't such a bad idea then or now.

He had no insight into what he would encounter in the morning but for the time being Simon felt great joy. He was finally going to get his chance. Finish what he started so many years ago.

He barely notices the cold breeze sneaking in through the button holes in his jacket as he walked the three blocks home. He wasn't even aware of the numbness in his hands or the pricking on the tops of his exposed ears. His beloved chair didn't get a second glance as he walked through the living room on his way up stairs and for the first time in years flopped down on his king size bed and slept the sleep of the old and satisfied, fully clothed, farting into the darkness of his room until the noises of the city getting up for work would wake him from his stinky tomb.

DAY ONE

Simon had imagined that his destination that morning was going to be somewhere in down town Detroit. His conjecture was based on how familiar Nick had been with the city and the fact that the Hummer was from the car pool at the "office". He never in a million years thought that they would be headed anywhere but to some inner city hide away. Some tall glass building, with two sided elevators, ones that went to the normal offices and ones that went to the not so normal. Those not so normal were the offices of the government of the United States. The same ones that Simon spent his days flipping through paper work in, waiting for the cake, the kiss and the gold watch that told him his services would no longer be needed. They were in every city in North America and some other continents not to be mentioned. Oh ya, on first glance they looked like any other office, people in little cubicles going about their corporate day. You had to look close to see the difference. It was in the eyes. Normal office protocol would suggest that during the mundane every day office routine the common employee would figure out the slack. Find a way to cheat the system. Maybe a little coffee time here, some under the radar phone calls to friends there, it all added up to time off the clock. You could see the eyes flitting about, looking for the next easiest distraction. Not here, not in these cubicles. Here there were intent stares, a hushed silence that was more indicative of a Remembrance Day minute that an office building and an almost palatable energy perched in wait for a call to action.

So when Nick turned south out of the city, Simon thought that maybe the office was in one of the numerous bedroom towns that surrounded the great city. Urban sprawl was a bi-product of any big center and Detroit was no different. The Canadian city of Windsor could almost be called a bedroom town. Many Motor City workers resided in Windsor. Not just because of the proximity but because of the housing.

Canadian housing was on par with the American but the neighborhoods could not compare. Where a home for $200,000.00 in Detroit was surrounded by gangs and hoodlums, a Canadian contemporary was surrounded with parks and government funded programs for stay at home moms. For the short commute across the border every day, what father or mother wouldn't want safety for their child over a twenty minute closer commute to work.

Simon's assumption on their destination was getting more wrong by minute as the suburban homes south of Detroit disappeared in the rear view mirror and they made their way south for more than forty minutes. Simon had been staring out the window at the Great Lake Erie so when they turned right off highway 75 onto a small side road his confusion as to their destination became even more so. They had traveled the side road about fifteen minutes when he noticed a little air field on his right. It was made even smaller by the large private jet parked at the end of the only runway.

Munroe Air Field was sandwiched between a ball park and the road. It was a haven for the weekend pilot and the first time parachutist struggling to get over their fear of heights and jumping out of a perfectly good plane. The jet sitting idling at the end of the runway was conspicuous in its lack of identification and the fact that it was idling. No one with a budget would idle a plane that size if they had any idea of what a gallon of jet fuel cost.

Simon knew immediately that this was not going to be a short day of getting re-acquainted with times past but a whole new indoctrination into the twenty first century.

As they pulled through the side gates of the airstrip and onto the tarmac of the runway Simon decided to go with it. The jet looked expensive and the fact that they were pulling right up to the gangway without having to pass any kind of airport security, big or small, meant this was not going to be his usual day at work. Nick was acting like it was an everyday event and as they went from the car to the jet Simon just followed along like nothing was out of the ordinary, even though his heart was going a mile a minute and he was pretty sure he was going to have to pee as soon as they got in the air.

There was no pre-flight safety spiel from the one and only flight attendant. They just chose whatever lazy boy recliner was nearest and sat down. The pilot wasn't wasting any time either. They were taxiing before Simon could get his safety belt done up and were in the air in what seemed like seconds. Once off the ground Nick explained to Simon that they were meeting the heads of state so to speak, the heads of SDI. That meant Washington DC. The usual flight time from Detroit to DC was just over an hour but they would probably make it in forty five. Special air space clearance would fast track them straight in to Regan National.

As his heart rate came down to normal, Simon could see that this was not an ordinary, run of the mill, private jet. It had been many years since he had been in the air. The last time he was inside an aircraft he had flown from Nevada to New York City in a Boeing 377 Stratocruiser. That was in 1955. The damn thing had propellers on it for Christ sake. He had been called to New York to go over the new design for the projectile they would be testing later in the year in Nevada. They had had a tough time trying to figure out how to rotate the interior of the projectile to compensate for the dramatic new rifling they had built into the walls of the exhaust well that compressed the plasma charge they were using to try and blast it into space.

Quantum theory's had been explored since the mid-twenties and though they still hadn't proved that their Thunder Well experiment could propel an object to escape velocity, some of the brains in the crowd were muddying up the process with ideas that the internal compartment of the projectile, turning at a counter rate to the ectoskin, could quite possibly set of a quantum event that would force the payload not into space but into the future.

Simon chuckled under his breath and Nick cast a quick glance in his direction. He came back from his revelry to the beautiful leather bound sofas and wrap around arm chairs of the main cabin. There was a TV built into the bulk head in front of him that was big enough that you could see the nose hairs of the news casters doling out the daily dose of misery and poor weather.

It was crazy; you could barely hear the engines. His fridge made more noise. He could still conjure up the horrendous rattle and bang of the old Boeing and remembered how he had a buzzing in his ears for a couple of hours after landing.

Almost as they reached altitude the jet started to descend. The air traffic guys at Regan were making a hole for them and they were even going to bypass the usual holding pattern of other flights so they could drop right in and to their hangar. Nick had taken the opportunity to nod off. The jet was as smooth as silk. No bumping or quick little stomach flipper on approach. You could have slept through the whole thing but Nick came to attention about ten feet off the ground. It was if he sensed it in his sleep and came too just in time to land.

The traffic at that time of day in DC was minimal and they arrived at the Mayflower Hotel in less than twenty minutes hangar to door.

The Mayflower, DC's oldest hotel still held some old world charm. The opulent main lobby with its upper lounge area and huge crystal chandeliers welcomed the guest with beaming bell hops and just enough rotting wood to make you think that Robert E Lee would pop out from behind the front counter to welcome you in.

The lobby bar wasn't open for service but Simon thought if it was, he just might have a belt to steady his nerves.

Nick and Simon strolled through the lobby, passing the elevators as they headed into the conference area of the main hall. The polished granite floor came up to meet then as they turned into a small enclave at the end of the building that serviced the spa area and the cleaning staff.

They took the maintenance elevator down three floors which brought them out into what looked and smelled like the maintenance basement then straight out of the elevator and through an adjacent walkway to a small unassuming wooden door in the hall.

When the door closed behind him Simon was taken back twenty years. It was the old sweat tank of the fifties. Nick left him standing just inside the door to let the brass know they had arrived and Simon took a moment to take the place in.

There were huge screens along one wall with what looked like satellite tracking and an extraordinarily beautiful view of earth from space.

Computers were in abundance. Hundreds of them, everywhere you looked someone was busy pecking away.

But it wasn't the scenery that took him back; it was the smells and the sounds.

An aura of starch from pressed white shirts and coffee on the brew with just an under lying hint of sweat and fear combined with muffled voices hushed in secretive conversations.

It was crazy but after all these years Simon could still feel the angst in the air. Not fear of the unknown, not even the sort of fear that would come with being in danger. No, it was that same old fear of having someone getting the jump on you, finding a solution that you should have seen, falling behind the bell curve at the office, losing your place in the corporate line.

It never fucking ended. No wonder they couldn't come up with a viable defense plan. Everyone was so busy playing office politics that they probably didn't have time to do any real research. He just shook his head and waited for Simon to come back and escort him to his meeting.

His escort was all smiles when he returned. Simon's nerves had calmed. This was familiar territory. He knew this game. It might have been a while since he had strapped on a glove but he could still play and by the look of things the rules hadn't changed very much.

They trailed through what seemed an almost endless line of desks. All in a row and every one manned with a geek. You could tell they were geeks. Each one spit polished and functioning at 110 percent. Simon could almost see the tension headaches welling up under the shirt collar of every one of them.

When they finally walked through the doors of the inner office it was as if a weight had been lifted. The air was cooler and sweeter and the noise was nonexistent as soon as the door closed behind them.

Nick and Simon walked into a very informal setting. Two leather couches, which looked like they had been commandeered from the hotel upstairs, were set in an L shape with a coffee table in the center and four other comfortable, high backed arm chairs between. A pot of coffee sat on the table along with a large urn of water sweating into a saucer and napkin. There were five men on the couch and they all rose to greet the two new members.

"This is Simon Harris" Nick announced and then proceeded to introduce the executive.

Jim Baker, research. Mark Robinson, procurement. Bill Nelson, robotics. Jim Evans, engineering. Barry Richardson, chemical & viral.

Simon guessed he was the lone nuke guy in the group.

There was only one in a suit, Mark, Simon figured he had to deal with people outside the building on a daily basis so he had to look the part. The rest were pretty casual. Jeans and kakis looked to be the dress code.

"Welcome Simon and thanks for moving so quickly on this." Jim Baker moved to the edge of the couch as he spoke.

"We have contacted your branch office and they are aware that you have been re-assigned. They don't know where or to what project and we would like to keep it that way. I'll just go over some of the ground rules before we get into the project and what we think you can bring to the table. First, can I get you a cup of coffee, it's pretty good. They send it down in a dumb waiter from the coffee shop upstairs."

Simon said "thanks" and leaned in to take the cup.

"First up, you're not in prison here. This is a research facility and we think that given your back ground you will likely spend more time in the field than in here. We will require that we meet here if there is anything that needs all heads involved. Your research is yours and you can pick up where you left off and you have full access to any resource we have no questions asked. You will have to make progress reports but we don't need pages of tech crap that takes forever to read. Just updates on progress. We are looking for results so the sooner you can get started the better. As Nick has probably told you we are on a timeline.

Simon looked to the faces of the group to see if there was any reaction to Jim's last comment. There was none.

"You have a room booked here under your own name and you can access it any time through the elevator that you came down on. You don't have to check into the hotel we will supply you with your key after the meeting.

You can go home any time you want and you have access to the jet to do so. Nick here will set you up with that any time you need.

You have any resource at your fingertips including money. We don't want you looking at costs just get results.

Call us by our first names. I hate being Mr. something or sir or any of that shit.

We have prepared an office and a lab area and we have a vehicle at your disposal 24/7. Don't hesitate to ask for anything you require. Now do you have any questions?"

Sounded like he could do whatever he friggin well wanted around here but Simon's first question was.

"So what Nick has told me is true? There are extra-terrestrials and they are hostile and we are kinda at war?"

"That is correct Simon. And we hope you can come up with something to give us an advantage in that war. Because we've been working on it for a long time and nothing has proved out no matter how much money we throw at it. So we're hoping you can give us an old school advantage. Otherwise we are just about out of ideas."

Simon sat in silence for a few seconds.

"What's my time line?" he asked.

"Just over twelve months"

That was the first time anyone other than Jim had opened his mouth. Mark Robinson spoke with a nice Texas drawl. Not overly drawn out, just enough to let you know where he came from. On any other given day he probably could have made a killing doing Ram Truck commercials.

"Give or take." He continued.

"When we finally broke the wow code it wasn't precise to the day as to when the event will take place. The brains in analysis think it's because our friends in space aren't exactly sure how long it's going to take them to make the trip."

Simon let that sink in for a second or two.

"Ok, my next question is why? What's their motivation? It seems like a hell of a long way to come just to be a bully."

"You have good reason to ask those questions. We asked that too. We are not so worried about the rhyme or reason but how many and what is their technology. The crux is that they know we are here and now we know they are there but who knows what, is the big question.

They may have as little Intel on us as we have on them. They might just be blowing smoke to scare us into giving up whatever it is they want from us. Could be the biggest bluff in the universe but if it isn't we want to be two steps ahead when the get here."

It sounded like a whole shit load of what ifs to Simon but quite frankly he could have given a shit one way or the other. He was back in the game and feeling like he was forty again.

"Ok, well, I'm in. I mean I really wasn't liking what I was doing in DC any way. Can I start by just talking to each of you and getting to know your end of the system and then I can dig up my old research and see if we can bring it into the twentieth century."

Bill Nelson stood up.

'Sounds like a good place to start to me. How about you grab your coffee and I'll give you the grand tour of the place.

Then you can settle into your office. Our names and numbers are already programmed into your phone so just call us up when you ready."

"Sounds good." Simon said, standing up himself.

Before he turned to follow Bill out onto the main floor, Simon turned to Nick.

"Thanks Nick. The whole thing still seems a bit far-fetched but it's already a lot more fun than the office in Detroit and the Paddy every night."

Nick just laughed. "The fun has just started my friend."

OLD TIMES

Simon's first impressions of the place were ones of familiarity. As he followed Bill around the facility it was just like old times. Seeing the row of heads bent over computer screens brought back memories, except his memories were of heads bent over computer print outs in his day. The florescent lights blazing down from somewhere in the white stippled drop ceiling, so many that there was an audible hum. Even the combination of copy toner, coffee and sweat in the air were the same.

The central office consisted of about twenty cubicles each with its desk and body. The back of the room extended out on either side of a wide hallway with what looked like individual lab areas. Every lab had a team, fully engrossed in what they were doing. All equally clad in the traditional white lab coat. It reminded Simon of a bunch of white lab rats only difference was here there was no prize if you got out of the maze.

The facility seemed larger than the floor above and Simon asked his tour guide about it.

"Yes, the area extends out under the street and we are also occupying the basement of the building next door. We thought it prudent to have two exits just in case. You have to remember we have been here for some time."

Clearly he had not taken into consideration that the Government would have immediately claimed the wow signal a threat and started to take steps to nullify that threat the second they felt in harm's way. He had really been in his own little world for the last three decades.

"Do you have a lab area set up for me? He asked.

"All set and ready when you are." Bill said.

"What about my old research? Is there any way to get our hands on that? I tried for a long time to get clearance to the files but I could never get through the red tape. When they shut me down in 57 they locked the stuff up tight and I never got another look at it. Over the years I tried to reconstruct the math and the ideas but it wasn't just me working on the project and I couldn't recall everything. The other guys had been told to keep quit if they were ever asked so I never did get back to square with what we had achieved back then."

Bill stopped mid stride and turned to Simon.

"Look Simon, we both know how the game goes. Everybody looks out for number one. If you see something coming down the pike that is going to affect your job or you position. You squash it, hide it or shred it. Whatever you have to do to keep working right? This time I think you'll be surprised. We have all your old material. Diagrams, math, even reclaimed some of the old holes you dug back in the day.

It's all piled in your lab area. It's up to you to dig through and get what you need to start new. Just let us know what you want besides that."

"All right, let's get too it then." Simon could barely contain himself.

They moved about half way down the row of labs where Bill opened one of the pneumatic doors with what looked like an everyday room key. As a matter of fact as he took a second look it did have the name of the hotel planted right on the front just like one of the hundreds that patrons used every day to access their rooms on the floors above.

"Now this key will get you into your lab and your room upstairs. I suggest you find some way to distinguish your lab. They all look the same and until you get used to where you are going you will find yourself out in the hall without a paddle so to speak. You can open no other lab with this key and the codes are changed every day when you access your door to leave your room. Your room information is on your desk. Dial 0 to get any equipment you need. Your old research is in the crates on the floor. That's it, have fun."

With that Bill opened the door to what would become Simons second home, held it until he had gone inside and without another word turned and walked back down the hall and away.

THE WELLS

That had been ten months ago. Since then Simon had reclaimed a couple of his old team mates and research buddies from the fifties and acquired a few new ones.

Most of the old squad had either died or were in situations where they had removed themselves from the kind of work Simon needed them to do but Sam and Larry couldn't wait to come out of retirement to help out and were even more incredulous when they were told what they would be doing.

The newbie's were part of the staff that already occupied the basement of the Mayflower but had the skills Simon was looking for to bring his project up to speed.

While his old work mates preferred the blue jeaned, shirt tail out look of the sixties the young blood came to work every day with their pants creased and the lab coat laundered. It was interesting to see the generations interact.

Simon's friend and recruiter, Nick, had come to the team after only a few days. Simon had an idea that Nicks particular skill set would come in handy. With his genetics and biological background Nick would develop a virus of some kind something flu driven, a nasty little bugger that would do more than give you a runny nose. Then they would combine the flu with a nanite of their own creation along with a projectile to deliver the whole nasty mess. Nanorobotics was not something that everyone and their dog knew about. If fact no one knew about it. Simon had stumbled onto some research back at the plant a year ago that had at the time seemed almost fantastical until one of his co-workers gave him a brief synopsis on the technology before warning him to keep clear of the whole thing if he know what was good for him. Back then Simon was just trying to get to pension without losing his spot against the wall at the Paddy. What he had seen was the first generation of an emerging technology field creating machines or robots whose components were close to the scale of a nanometer ($10-9$ meters) more specifically, nanorobotics or nanomites.

One of the first useful applications of nanomachines might be in medical technology, where it could be used to identify and destroy cancer cells.

For Simons purpose this kind of miniature robot cold crawl into anything no matter how tightly screwed down and carry a virus along with it infecting everything that it came in contact with.

If they could get the general blast theory to work correctly he was going to try a twofold defense plan. Both payloads would be delivered using atomic detonation. Atomic being the lesser of the nuclear reactions would force the shell carrying the pathogen into space. Specifically, 650 miles above the earth to the fifth layer of atmosphere the exosphere. Here the projectile would release billions of nanites, nanites so small that even the most air tight structure would not be safe from infection. Each infused with a special form of influenza; they would fly into the solar winds that would spread them out in waves. Nick had been working on a particularly virulent form of the flu. One that would essentially cause the lungs to fill with so much mucous that anyone or anything that became infected would literally drown in their own fluids. The flu would be bonded to the nanites and the nanites would be programmed to release the pathogen the instant that it came in contact with and attached itself to any object. Essentially anything in that space would be contaminated and anything that wanted to get to earth would have to come through that space. That included meteorite material. No one was worried about that as once a meteor entered the mesosphere the virus would burn up along with its host. The genetic makeup of the flu had also been programmed to become dormant at forty thousand feet earth atmosphere.

The second part of the plan was to give the flu some time to infect the invaders so they were unable to react to any attack from earth and then from the same launch wells send projectiles carrying war heads with enough thermonuclear force to evaporate anything for thousands of miles, aliens and the remaining virus alike.

Seamed like a pretty simple plan to Simon and in the last few months most of the bugs had been ironed out of the idea. They had poured over all the old paper work and were basically back to the point where the project had been shut down. They had figured out how to keep the two rotating parts of the delivery system from creating an electromagnetic charge that could potentially short circuit the nanites by using an old school method of coating one of the cylinders in glass. The initial G force was counteracted by simply filling the void between the outer casing and the glass delivery system inside with water. Cylinder structure was held up by the use of what the old boys liked to call flying buttresses, external wings that not only acted as guidance and stability but kept the external part of the casing from expanding or contracting due to stress and temperature change. The only thing left was to test fire one of the wells with the new shells to fine tune the intricate rotations, both externally and internally. They had to make sure the payload would not be destroyed by the force of the detonation and that the inner shell would remain static during the blast.

There were other aspects of the world wide vision that included all nuclear nations to dedicate a certain number of their nukes not just as strike force but to powering the delivery systems. That, however, was a hurdle they would leave until they knew the physics' were sound.

So almost a year after his encounter with Nick in the old Paddy, Simon stood on a mountain side in Wyoming. Glad to be out of the Washington basement that had quickly become like a jail. The crisp mountain air felt cleansing as it flowed through his nostrils and filled his lungs.

This was the same place he had stood so many years before. The well they had dug then was now re-formed and re-calibrated. The iron walls had been given specific rifling so to send its projectile spinning into space at an amazing velocity. As he exhaled he imagined expelling all the stress that had come with developing his program and as he moved to enter the bunker that contained the detonator for the first experimental firing of the Thunder Well he momentarily reflected on the years in between, remembering the failures while bracing for victory.

LAUNCH

Simon closed and sealed the door that led into the control center under the mountain. From outside you would had to have known exactly where it was and what the trigger was to open the door. There were camouflaged guards stationed at various points along the old logging road that led to the bunker and video surveillance was hardwired to heaven. A phrase used by Simon's team which meant that from ground level to satellite they had twelve thousand miles of visibility.

The bunker itself was on the west side of the mountain and the Thunder Well was east. Even though this part of Wyoming was government owned, no one was allowed with in twenty miles at detonation and within thirty miles of blast after. The team had worked long and hard on a solution to the fallout and the destructive power of the bomb. The damage to the integrity of the well was not so much an issue as the holes were easy to dig and once fitted and armed could be within two miles of each other. Wells could be dug, rifled and fitted in four days.

The real issue was the fallout. After hundreds of hours and thousands of lab tests the solution came down to wadding.

In the 1800's wadding was used in musketry to seal the gases created in a gun barrel at firing from the projectile, creating greater force in the barrel and giving the bullet greater velocity.

A Thunder Well was designed in three parts.

1. The Blast Hole

This was the bottom third of the shaft that contained the explosive. Here the detonation took shape and had its force directed up the shaft.

2. Contact

This was the middle third of the shaft where the energy of the blast met the wadding below the projectile and started forcing it up the well.

3. The Rifle

This was the top third of the shaft that contained the steal casing that gave the projectile its rifling or spin before it saw the light of day.

The Thunder Well was deep enough that though the detonation and force were extreme, the projectile had literally outrun the wadding and the blast by the time it reached the casing at the top of the well.

Every shell had its own laser signal. As the shell left the shaft a small receiver in the well head picked up the laser signal and slammed shut a twenty ton steal cap before the original blast could escape, at the same time flooding the blast hole with water to counteract any blowback from the initial blast. The resulting encased radioactive fallout was trapped in the well to be cleaned at a later time.

As Simon walked down the cement corridor that led to the main control center he began to hear the hum of human and electrical occupation ahead. The air became warmer and a bit close as he stepped from the bare concrete to the carpeted arena that held the steady satellite image of the east side of the mountain. Big eight foot screens covered one wall and desks had been set up in a semi-circle to maximize the view. Other than his immediate team there were the original five from his interview. Jim Baker, Mark Robinson, Bill Nelson, Jim Evans and Barry Richardson, all on hand to slap each other on the back in success or be the first to point fingers and cover their asses if not.

Barry and Simon had not been friends. Barry basically thought Simon had stolen Nick, who was originally assigned to his team, away from what Barry thought a more important area of research. Simon could have cared less but Barry made a point of avoiding Simon's requests for anything and he had not shown up at any of Simons briefings before today. Simon could only surmise that Barry was there to gloat in case of failure. A few security personal and a couple of electricians made up the balance of the group huddled in the hole under the Wyoming Rocky Mountains.

Simon surveyed the group and then pulled open the back pack he had been wearing. There were a couple of surprised laughs as he pulled out an old 1930's magneto.

Simon had made arrangements to fly to Detroit so he could pack a few things for the test firing. One of the items that came with him was an old magneto styled plunger, a piece of history almost forgotten except for old western films starring Gene Autry or John Wayne where some cowboy was blowing up the train or taking down the side of a mountain in search of gold.

Simon had purchased it at an estate auction for no other reason than what it represented in history and because he liked the look of it.

The magneto was heavy. Made out of solid pine, the two terminals still in good shape and ready to go, the plunger pulled out in anticipation. He had had the guts reworked back in the sixties so it was in working condition and could still generated a spark.

The firing mechanism for today's test was simple. Just two terminals with a switch covered by an opaque plastic cap to keep someone from accidentally firing the weapon before it was time.

Simon nodded one of the nearby electricians over.

"You do the work on this place or just here in case we need a wrench turned?"

"Nope, I worked on it for most of this year. I can tell you where every circuit is connected and where the turds go when you flush the toilet." He said with a grin.

Simon got a good chuckle out of that one. At least someone here had a sense of humor.

"Well then you're the guy I need. Can you pull the detonator switch apart and make it work with this?" Simon said pulling the magneto into view.

"Wow! That's a beauty. Nineteen thirties, right?"

"Yup" Simon replied. "Think you can make her work?"

"If not I'll buy the beers."

Simon quickly realized that there would be no free beers this day. The tech had the detonator flip switch disconnected, re-routed and wired into the magneto in about 45 seconds.

This was a guy Simon needed to remember.

As he turned to the team he was met with varied expressions. Those he had worked with for the past year had already started to check out the old box with its red handled plunger. The others could only be described as "not impressed"

Simon didn't have time to explain to the grumpy bunch that man had been trying to blast objects into orbit since the 17th century. It wasn't a new concept. The worst that could happen here would be a huge hole in the ground and they would have to recalibrate. Might as well have a little fun while they were ate it.

The magneto connected Simon strolled the bank of ten computer monitors set up in front of the big screens, stopping at each station to make the final checks. This wasn't rocket science. There wasn't astronaut lives at stake here. It worked or it didn't. If it did, on to phase two, if not, back to the drawing board. Although, Simon thought, they were running out of time for drawing.

Checks in order, all systems go. Simon turned to Nick who sat at the last computer station.

"Would you like to do the honors Nick"

Simon could tell by the grin on Nicks face he wouldn't have to convince him.

"Thanks Simon" was all he said.

"Gentlemen and ladies" Simon began. "Even though we are a safe distance away from the blast hole and separated by a mile of bedrock, there will be a shock wave associated with detonation. For those of you who have never seen or been witness to a nuclear blast, there will be a concussion some moments after detonation. Please know that this is normal and nothing to be concerned about. Be more concerned if you feel nothing."

With that Simon turned to Nick and just nodded. The room had become eerily quiet. The high pitched wine of the magneto as Nick pushed the plunger home seemed almost absurd.

The plunger hit bottom and still silence. The giant monitors with the video and satellite angles stood motionless. There was an audible sound of dissatisfaction from the group of observers who had obviously expected an immediate reaction to the plunger meeting is zenith.

Then, just as some started to turn away from the screens, a huge cloud of white gas and debris flew from the mouth of the launch site. Unlike most atomic clouds instead of mushrooming into the air and sending out an ecclesiastic, it projected straight into the air and then as the blast door slammed shut over the launch chamber, its root cut from its length, it proceeded to climb for a couple of miles before losing its impetus and dissipating quite benignly.

Those watching from the back of the room had started to applaud when the impact of the blast hit. Not earthquake scary but enough to move the floor beneath their feet and shut them up pretty damn quick.

Simone turned to the group.

"No worries ladies and gentlemen" he said, "That shock wave was expected as I said. What we really want to applaud is if the satellite's pick up the shell leaving the first layer of atmosphere. That will be success."

"Shouldn't that only be a few seconds?" One of the bystanders asked.

"Actually it might take a few minutes for the satellites to hone in on the shell. They have always been programmed for much larger targets. We should get some results in about two minutes if the projectile didn't evaporate in the well."

Now all attention was focused on the screens. A video replay of the launch was looping on one. Playing the fifteen second span that had captured the detonation. It was virtually impossible to tell if the payload had left the well. If it had it was traveling at a rate that the human eye was unable to see.

Then, there it was, the satellite system had correlated the trajectory and speed of the object and was tracking its progress into space.

"Can you zoom to any degree on the shell?" Simon asked the sat tech on terminal three.

"Yes, we can get about ten percent before we would lose visual contact. Anymore and we would have to track with ground telescopes which would be very difficult."

"Let's do it then. Take it in just far enough so I can see if we have rotation."

"Ok," the tech replied. "Zooming one point, two points, three points …"

As the tech counted down the zoom Simon strained into the screen. As the count got to five he began to get a clear sense of motion from the object screaming across the sky.

"Six points, Seven Points" came the count.

"Ok, hold it right there." Simon said.

If he was asked it would have been very difficult for Simon to share his thoughts at that moment. There on the screen, clearly rotating through the atmosphere was the shell, undamaged by the blast, hurtling toward its destination in the exosphere. He felt like crying and laughing at the same time. After forty two years his dream, his project had succeeded. There was still the release of the payload to complete the mission but as far as Simon was concerned he felt vindicated and alive.

Simon turned to the room.

"That ladies and gentlemen is a successful launch."

All the tension in the room was gone as the cheers went up. Simon looked over at Nick who gave him the two thumbs up.

"We still have the delivery of the payload to be completely successful, but that will not be for just over an hour so let's celebrate the success of the launch and get ready for the second phase."

As Simon spoke chairs grated back and technicians slapped each other on the back. Some of these people had not seen their homes and families more than twice in the last year. The five of the executive team moved to congratulate Simon.

"Great work" Bill Nelson extending his hand.

"Yes, it was a long time coming." Simon responded. "We still have a couple of hurdles to leap before we are done today but that was a great first success."

"I'm not sure what you mean." Jim Baker of research seemed confused.

Simon had only used the top executives in his research and development when he had no one else to go to. Not because they were incompetent or too bureaucratic to get the job done but because they just asked too many questions and held up everyone else up while they justified the requests made of them. So when Jim said he wasn't sure what Simon had meant by more to be done, it didn't frustrate him in the least. Simon had deliberately kept them in the dark on most of the project so he could get it done within the time lines he had been given.

"Well," Simon replied. "There are two other parts of this mission that still need to complete. One, and probably the more important of the two, is the checking of the well. We need to make sure not only that the blast door contained the fallout but that the chamber flooded properly to absorbed the contamination. Second, once the delivery system reaches the exosphere, we need to make sure it can deliver the payload into the solar winds. The shell we launched today has a thousand miniature tracking bacons that we will release to the winds for study. That will tell us how to prepare the viral nanites for maximum effect."

"Shouldn't that be an easy thing? Releasing the payload?

Jim Evans had helped with some of the engineering problems they had had with the flying buttresses but had not been in on the final planning of the delivery system. It was simple, the ectoskin or the outer layer of the shell was designed to disintegrate at approximately fifty five thousand miles an hour. That would leave the glass internal shell that carried the pathogen coated nanites exposed. The carbon internal shell that carried the nanites was full of microscopic holes, big enough for the little buggers to escape. Once the glass was exposed to even the small atmosphere of the exosphere the glass would melt letting the nanites escape.

"Why are there two shells?" Bill asked.

"Essentially, the outer shell is rotated by the rifling in the well so it maintains its trajectory. The inner glass shell is programmed to rotate counter clock wise to offset the outer rotation. This keeps the payload from heating up and destroying the pathogen before it can be released." Simon explained.

It was obvious none of these guys had given the project much hope. It was rumored around the lab that the brass had been dubious as to the validity of re-visiting a forty year old idea that had found its birth before the age of sophisticated computers. They had probably had a few laughs at Simon's expense over the last year but no one was laughing right now. They were scrambling to get up to speed and Simon didn't have time to brief them.

"All this information is in my weekly reports which I believe everyone got a copy off. I do have the research on hand and can give you access to a computer if you have any other questions but right now I have work to do. Please excuse me while I talk to my team"

With that Simon left the group open mouthed and somewhat embarrassed but he didn't give a shit. If the next phase of the launch didn't worked it wouldn't be because he hadn't done his homework.

PHASE TWO

The next forty five minutes Simon had no time for questions. The launch data was pouring in and though most of it was expected Simon didn't want to miss any small anomaly that could lead to disaster in the second half of the experiment.

Nick was close at his shoulder the whole time. This next half hour would tell the tale as to whether Nicks micro mechanisms were going to do the job or not. Neither was concerned about the virus Nick had concocted. It was the functioning of the delivery system that was making them sweat. Hell anyone could develop a virus. All you needed was some particularly virulent snot. Didn't even have to be human. No, it was the disbursement of the nanites, the small DNA based machines that would be the most important piece of this puzzle.

They watched the satellite feed as the projectile began to enter its targeted range. The nanites that the inner glass carried on this mission had been infused not with a viral flu, but with a florescent coating that the satellite would be able to detect. Not individually but more like an Aurora Borealis curtain expanding as the solar winds swept them along.

Suddenly there it was shimmering across the screens like a fairy waving its wand over the sky in a Disney movie.

Simon was suddenly very tired. It was like he had been holding his breath for forty years.

Nick saw Simon's reaction and almost reached out to support the older man who had become his friend.

"Not the time for slacking off." Nick whispered in Simon's ear.

"To many looking for a reason to move us out now that they know this works."

That was all Simon needed to snap him back to the present and the project. No one was getting in his way this time.

As the glittering wave expanded across the screens the group of scientists and technicians huddled in the mountain core finally took the time to congratulate themselves on a job well done. Backs were slapped, strangers were hugged and cigars were lit, a time honored tradition that had its roots in the early days of NASA.

Simon participated freely in the handshakes and the hugs. He was particularly surprised when one of his much younger female colleagues hug came with a pretty good ass grabbing.

Simon hadn't had his ass handled by a female for so long he wasn't quite sure how to take it. He knew one thing for sure, if he thought about it too long he would have to sit down so he wouldn't have to tell everyone that it was probably the radiation that had made his penis a bit bigger.

WAR ROOM

The week following the testing of the Thunder Well was spent mostly crunching numbers. Everything added up. The defense system that Simon had envisioned would work. Now they just needed to answer the questions that inevitably came with success.

How long would it take to make enough of the projectiles to defend Earth? How many holes could be dug and configured in what time frame? How long would it take to produce enough flu virus to infect an army and how long to manufacture the nanite army that would carry the weapon into space? The inevitable litany of uninformed queries that usually evolved into the back room politicking of the Washington elite. It was a wonder to Simon that humans had come so far. For a brief moment, in the middle of some Senators blathering, Simon thought, maybe an Alien invasion is just what the world needed to get rid of some of these jack asses.

In the midst of all the inquiries Simons mind kept returning to the ass grabbing he had endured at the hands of one of his lab techs.

It would seem that it hadn't been just an over exuberant display of joy at the success of the launch. He had run into the tech a couple of times in the following week and both times the girl had seemed more than interested in him. He had found out that her name was Kim. She had been working on the project for about eight months mostly on the flu side with Nick but she was also a controller, keeping tabs on all the data that came in on a daily basis. That would explained why Simon hadn't noticed her he thought, but she had actually read some of Simons papers from the first experimental wells and knew a lot about him. She even knew where he lived and some personal stuff that Nick had told her, like his favorite bar was a place in Detroit called the Paddy for Christ sake.

She was in her late thirties or early forties Simon thought and he wondered what the hell she could possibly see in an aging physicist with very little future outside this one event.

That being said it might be one event for everyone. That brought a smirk to his face.

He was just mulling these thoughts over when around the corner the object of his thoughts, Kim, came hurrying, head down and it looked to Simon in somewhat of a panic.

As she came rushing past Simon turned in her direction.

"Hello" he said.

Kim jumped at the sound of his voice, obviously engrossed in the paperwork she had been staring at as she hurried through the lab; she hadn't even noticed he was standing there.

"Oh" she exclaimed, "Simon, sorry, I was going over some information and I have been so caught up in this damn thing I don't think I have come up for air in a couple of days."

"Well, you should take a couple of breaths and maybe we can get a coffee?" Simon replied.

"Actually, I will take you up on that and while we're at it, I want to go over something I found that is quite disturbing and I am not sure if it's a mistake or a deliberate bit of sabotage."

"Well then let's make this a coffee for three and take Nick with us."

"Good idea. Can you give him a call and invite him to join us?"

Simon grabbed the phone on a nearby desk and dialed Nick's number which over the past year he had committed to memory. When he answered, Simon asked him to take a break and to meet them upstairs in the lobby bar of the hotel. Nick's answer was immediate and Kim and Simon quickly stepped into the elevator and headed up to the lobby.

The lobby bar of the Mayfair hotel in Washington DC had seen its fair share of dignitaries. It was also a great place to talk privately as the high ceilings, marble pillars and floors along with the general cacophony of the front lobby made it almost impossible for anyone to eaves drop on a conversation without actually sitting at the same table.

Nick arrived shortly after Kim and Simon sat down and the three ordered coffee from the waiter.

Nick looked from Kim to Simon. "What's up?" he inquired.

Your guess is as good as mine" Simon replied "I bumped into Kim in the lab or I should say she almost ran me over, and I am still in the dark as too the exact concerns she has."

Both men waited while Kim skimmed the top couple of letter sized printouts she was holding. When she finally looked up they could see that it wasn't so much a look of concern on her face but more on of puzzlement.

"Ok" she said. "I was going over the numbers from the test firing and as I was looking up data I could see that some of the results have changed from my original findings on the day. I made sure to take a backup of everything that was recorded digitally from the test firing not just the numbers but the video feeds from the ground and satellite imagery as well. I know it has changed because I checked most of the original results from that day to the ones I took myself. They originally synced up but as of yesterday they have been altered. If my set of files had of been immediately different form the project data then I would have said that there may have been an error on my part but since they initially were identical I can only assume that someone has sabotaged the findings. The weird thing is that if that is true, they didn't do a very good job of hiding the changes. I mean the alterations are almost in plain sight."

Both Nick and Simon looked at each other in surprise.

"Really" Nick said. "I mean who in their right mind would try to shut down this experiment when everyone knows the implications of doing so?"

"You know", Kim said, "I think Mark Robinson had his hand in this. He has been selectively absent from briefings and has all but refused to take part in this project since day one. He has personally voiced his opinion on Nick working for us and I wouldn't be surprised if he would love to see us fail, even at the risk of human annihilation."

"So how are the results altered?" Simon asked.

"It's in the rifling numbers for the bore holes. Someone has changed out the twist rates for the wells."

"As you know we spent months determining the exact twist so the outer skin of the projectile spun to the left, at the precise turn of the internal delivery system to the right. One point to either side ended up in a bubonic soup. Like the highest speed blender you would ever see. What our testing discovered was that the forward momentum of the projectile actually sped up the rotation of the internal delivery system so the rifling of the casing had to have an increased twist rate to speed up the rotation of the outer skin of the projectile as it passed through the well. In Rifling terms this is called a gain twist or progressive twist.

At any rate the calibrations for the rifling of the well casing were exact. Any deviation would result in the failure of the projectile and its payload. Someone, after our successful launch the other day, has gotten into the secure files and changed those rifling numbers. If I hadn't of written down the data as it came in during the test we could very well have created hundreds of wells with the wrong rifling and sent our defensive package into space with little or no effect. The fact that I double checked computer stats against what I had written down is pure luck and means that someone has tampered with the numbers since then."

Nick and Simon just stared at one another. Who in their right minds would screw with the last chance to ward off human annihilation?

It had been one of those things where all was focused on the technical and the obvious had gotten lost in the shuffle. They had spent all their waking hours developing the cause and the delivery system but had come up short in the initial trials because they couldn't figure out what was causing the inner capsule that was to carry the virus into the outer atmosphere, to rip its self in half or turn the viral body into a useless soup. It had not occurred to Simon that they would need some way of stabilizing the projectile both externally and internally, not only to keep its payload from become abused but to maintain a specific flight path for the entire package.

In the old days they hadn't really cared too much about where anything went after the initial detonations. They were more concerned with blast force and fall out than anything else. It wasn't until one of the giant well caps went missing after an explosion that they had even begun to consider the trajectory of anything that might get launched during one of their little test. Besides it was right around then that the project had been shut down so any thought of rifling the steel casings was really an idea brought to the table with this new project.

Simon had not thought about the old project for some time now and as he reminisced about how he had fought to keep it alive his old hatred of the system and the pompous asses that ran most of the experimental projects made his skin crawl. Here, decades after the fact the same ass covering, boot licking suck ups were at it again.

This time they were in for a surprise. Simon's idea of how to get a job done had changed. He no longer felt the need to go through the appropriate channels. He had been given a reprieve and he intended to use it to prove that his theories and ideas where valid, if not essential to mankind moving forward. Besides he had Nick and maybe Kim to push his ideas further than even he could have imagined. No, nothing was keeping him from accomplishing his goal this time. Not even some self-serving moron… Simon suddenly had a thought. What if this isn't some government sponsored sabotage? What if it's not some pro something faction that has somehow infiltrated their experimental group? What if this is one of them? An alien, planted in the most strategic possession so that no matter what earths defensive idea they would have a heads up?

Shit… that's it. That's what this is all about. We have an alien amongst us.

The realization that there was an alien dressed in human clothing was shocking but at the same time seamed totally plausible. Anyone trying to sabotage their experiments that knew anything would never just sneak into the secure computer system and change rifling codes. It had to be someone who was just observing developments and trying to delay the results.

What the hell, Simon though. Why? If you are going to wage war on a world what would you need most? Intel would be the obvious answer. The ability to know what the plan was. But was that it? The sabotage seemed so juvenile.

These thoughts took nano seconds to race through Simons mind.

As he snapped out of his revelry Simon noticed Nick looking at him.

"What", he said.

"Well." Nick said. "It looked like all the secrets of the ancient world just revealed themselves to you. So spill you guts, what were you thinking?

Simon took a moment. The twenty foot ceilings in the lobby seamed to shrink into a five foot box that surrounded the trio. Waiters came and went but like in a slow motion dream. Both Nick and Kim had leant in to catch Simon's words.

REVELATION

"I think I know what's going on here." Simon said. His hushed tone barely audible above the hubbub of the lobby and other surrounding conversations.

"I don't think this has ever been about invasion. At least not in the sense that we think of invasion. I think someone has taken the message and distorted its meaning or the meaning has been misread. Don't get me wrong, I think aliens are coming, but I think there is a conspiracy here that we don't fully understand."

"Well, I understand one thing." Nick said. "If I just spent a whole year and some days developing a virus that essentially comes down to a snot bomb, and now this whole thing is going to go all Kum Ba Yah? Well shit is gonna hit the fan."

"No, no, listen. I'm not saying the invasion isn't real. I'm just saying I think the target is not to destroy or take earth hostage. I think there is something else."

Simon paused to catch his breath. The things that were whirling around in his head were going to need more than a few drinks to sort out.

"Listen, Kim, get your data together. Include the recent changing of the figures. See if you can track the infiltration back to the originating computer." Nick turned to Simon.

"Simon, make sure we have some kind of security. I mean come up with a plan so only the three of us can share info. I mean, we have to make sure that no one outside the three of us can get hold of any information we dig up."

They agreed and made plans to meet again the next afternoon same time same place. Why was there always someone trying to throw a fuck into his projects Simon thought. This time should have been a no brainer. They were trying to save the world for Christ sake and some jack ass had an agenda. It never failed.

Simon left the hotel after saying good bye to Nick and Kim. He used the front door this time. He needed a change, some place with people, a place like the old Paddy back home, somewhere he could get a couple of drinks in without worrying about how drunk he got or who saw him doing it.

He didn't have to walk far. The Lucky Bar was a block up and on the same side of the street. Simon could hear the sound of a basketball game pounding out of a

bunch of TV's and since the door stood open wide to the street he could smell the stench of cheap booze and the working class perfume of a hard days labor, which always reminded him of Campbell's mushroom soup, and today reminded him of home and his usual corner in the Paddy Wagon. It was perfect. No one would care who he was and he knew no one would care what he did, at least not until they kicked his ass out at closing time.

Simon had found a great little table in a corner, his favourite place, back to the wall and had just started sipping his second Jim Beam and branch, when a familiar shadow blocked what remained of the daylight coming in through the open door.

He didn't look up and the shadow didn't ask if he could join. He just sat down.

"Thought I would find you here" Nick said. The smile in his voice was hard to hide.

"What made you think that?" Simon retorted. Not really unhappy to have some company.

"Well, I just hit the street and looked for the shittiest place in a one block radius. Wasn't really too hard." Nick was really having a hard time containing his laughter.

Simon's sense of humor was starting to return. He guessed he was pretty predictable.

"I was trying to find a place to give this whole sabotage idea some thought. It just seems a bit to contrived, maybe even a bit too easy. I mean, why someone would go into the computer and change our launch results is beyond me. More than that why would they do something so obvious? Unless they wanted us to find the changes and do what we are doing right now. Wondering why."

Nicks beer had come and he sucked half back in the first gulp.

"What is it your saying? Someone is trying to get our attention? Why and what is it they are trying to get us to understand, because if this is some kind of sabotage it's a pretty lame attempt.

"Exactly, Simon said, why do something so obvious and in such a way to make sure it was us that found the changes? It has to be someone who is close, close enough and knowledgeable enough about the project to be able to get the security codes to the data and understand who would immediately know that changes had been made."

Nick had plowed through his beer and the two sat in momentary silence while they waited for their drinks to be refreshed.

"Someone is trying to tell us something, Simon said, and I don't think it's about disrupting the project. I think it's about the real reason there is a project in the first place. Otherwise why wouldn't they have just erased the entire data base? If they have access to our protected files they surely know how to destroy them and the backups. No, this is something else."

"I agree, but what? I need a couple more beers to really get into this conspiracy thinking mode."

Nick had already downed the last order and waved the waitress over.

"Bring me a couple of those beers this time and if you have something besides bar tequila, bring me a shot of that as well."

Simon wasn't concerned about Nick's alcohol consumption. Since they had met Simon had witnessed Nick's ability to consume enough booze to render a normal man unconscious. Nick said when he was crunching numbers there was no room for alcohol but when he was trying to think he like to change his perspective a bit.

Nick's idea of a bit and Simons where two different things but essentially they ended up in the same place, pretty buzzed and really hung over the next day.

As the drinks started to calm the two down, napkins and coasters started to become game plans. Scenarios and what ifs written down in ballpoint became lengthier and lengthier as the drinks kept coming. Both Simon and Nick knew it was time to knock off the think tank when there last conspiracy theory ended up at the feet of Elvis.

They might not have accomplished a lot but they did have one good solid idea to take from the table full of empty glasses and used napkins. Someone was definitely trying to get their attention. They needed to look a little closer at the changes that were made to the launch data and figure out what it was they were supposed to see in the change.

CONSPIRACY

A thin ray of light poked its way through the tiniest of space in the curtains of Simon's hotel room. On any other day of the year the sun would have been just different enough in its arc to miss the little opening and it would have continued on its way until it sank behind the office building across from the Mayflower Hotel, never finding its way into Simon's domain.

On this particular day however, the pencil thin ray sliced through the darkened room coming to rest ever so gently on Simons closed right eyelid. It's gentle warmth belayed its intense brightness and was all that his sleeping, booze addled brain needed to start it's return to consciousness from the depths of a solid gold tequila filled sink hole.

As the jack hammers and the very low flying B52 that was Simons dehydrated neurotransmitters trying to make sense of consciousness, came to life, Simon made his first bad decision of the day.

I think I'll open one eye and see if it hurts, he thought. The right one feels pretty good so "open sesame"

As Simons retina, which was fully dilated behind the dark shield that was his eyelid, became aware of the screaming white sun light that had perfectly aligned itself through the hole in the curtain, it tried in vain to close itself down. The ensuing pain shot through his head like a smack from a pipe wrench, lifting him out of bed and leaving him sprawled and retching on the floor of his otherwise darkened room.

When the world came back to Simons addled mind he dragged himself into the bathroom, crawled into the tub and turned on the shower. That was his second bad decision of the day.

The water from the shower head in Simon's room wasn't freezing, not like if you cut a hole in an icy pond and jumped in, but it was cold enough to shock Simon's system with almost as much force as the brain piercing light ray had.

This time a whoosh of air escaped his mouth along with a fairly agonizing noise that was reminiscent of the moaning that comes with chronic pain.

He hadn't felt this shitty in a while. Not since he had taken on this new work. Oh sure, he had a couple of mornings that were close back in the days of the Paddy, but not in his time in Washington.

As the water heated up Simons hangover started to subside just enough for him to down a couple of pain killers while he sat letting the warmth of the water bring him back to the world.

He had just begun to wonder how the hell he had gotten home when the phone started to ring. It only took about thirty seconds of cursing to make it stop but only long enough for whoever was on the other end to call back.

A thick cotton towel only captured some of the water as Simon left a damp trail from the tub to the office desk that held the phone and numerous documents pertaining to the next phase of the Thunder Well testing.

With the phone cradled in his neck, Simon attempted to dry off as he abruptly answered.

"Make it good, cause I need to sleep."

"Ya, I saw Nick this morning." Kim's way to cheery voice exploded in his ear." Or I should say I saw the back of his head while he was peucking in his waist basket. What did you two do last night?"

"Just a little brain storming, which is why I can't talk right now, there's a storm in my brain."

"Well get it together sunshine, I think I may have a clue as to our saboteur or at least a lead in that direction."

"On my way." Simon said, not really knowing if he was or not.

The eight hundred milligrams of ibuprofen Simon had somehow got down his throat was starting to kick in. At least the buzzing in his head had come down to a mild hum and his eye didn't feel like someone had stuck a knitting needle in it any more.

He jumped back into the still running shower and cleaned up. No amount of toothpaste or mouthwash was going to straighten out what was going on in his mouth though. Fifteen minutes later he was exiting the tunnel that lead from the basement of the hotel to the facility that housed Thunder Well next door.

Kim greeted him with a wide grin. "It ain't that funny" Simon whined.

"Really?" She replied, and handed him what essentially was a very strong Bloody Mary.

Simon almost hurled at the smell of the vodka and tomato juice but force half of it down anyway.

"Let's get Nick and see what you found out. Is he able to function for this?"

"Oh, I gave him the same remedy when he got in an hour ago and he seems to be coming around. I already called him and we are meeting in your office right now."

Simon followed along like a chastised puppy, the neon lighting sounding like a swarm of cicadas in his head.

THE PLOT THICKENS

"Simon almost laughed when he caught his first glimpse of Nick through the glass of his office. He was white as a ghost and his usually natty attire was slightly wrinkled like he had slept in his office chair all night.

When Nick entered the office both Simon and Nick took one look at each other and burst out laughing. Almost simultaneously they both said,

"You look like shit" and burst out laughing again.

"If you two lovers can quit touching each other's bums long enough to sit down, I'll give you an update on what I found out last night while you were out on a Jose Cuervo pilgrimage." Kim didn't really sound too upset with them, but both thought they should at least try to concentrate enough to hear her out.

"Ok," she began," I think I might have found a clue, but I need your opinions as to whether it makes any sense or not. The only thing that was changed in all of the data from our test firing of the well was the twist rate of the barrel and the projectile length. Both necessary elements to get our projectile into space with its cargo intact. That in itself may seem like a good place to start if you are going to sabotage the project but one that would be caught very quickly and since the barrels have already been rifled, a change that even though modified in the data would not have affected the outcome. That made me wonder if the changes weren't meant to sabotage the testing but to get our attention. The two changes that were made where the projectile length, from 230 inches to 33.3 and the twist rate from 1045 to 104.5. Those are two very odd numbers, especially if you are trying to throw a wrench into the works. The more I looked at the numbers the more I knew they were meant for something other than to throw a wrench into project.

At first I thought it was two radio station call signs but after some investigation I found that 33.3 is not a viable signal and 104.5, while interesting, it is what it is, a Gospel radio station with Baptist roots.

Next I ran the numbers as if they were positions on the map. It was here I hit on something I think may be of some interest. The only other thing I could think that consisted of two different numbers in association with one another was GPS quadrants. My first attempt using 33.3 W and 104.5 N landed me just outside of Baltimore Maryland in the middle of an intersection in Glen Burnie. My second attempt, reversing the numbers to 33.3 N and 104.5 W came up with an interesting location.

At this point in the conversation neither Simon nor Nick had said a word. Though Kim's analysis had been simple and concise, the two men were finding it difficult to focus on the facts.

Kim had turned the computer monitor around to face the two half-baked scientists. That, I guess you could say, is what really hit the sober button. Both men straightened up and leaned in to the screen.

"What the hell?" Simon muttered.

"You got to be shittin me." Was Nick's expletive.

"I shit you not' Kim replied, "Those where a couple of the words that came to mind when I saw this too, along with a very bad feeling."

"How did you get this image?"

"The government satellite and GPS system. You know the guys we're working for. Remember we have access to every government and military asset in the good old USA and then some. I just used their tracking numbers and satellite to source out our little piece of the earth and voila!"

All three were staring at what were essentially an airport and its surrounding hangars out buildings and outlying properties. The GPS pinpoint was smack dab in the center point of what looked like a triangular shaped ditch its longest point facing east. Contained by a road on either side the geometric symbol was too perfect to miss.

What had elicited the response from Simon and Nick was not so much the triangle shape, which in itself was slightly more than interesting, but the name of the airport in which the shape was confined. That was what had brought them upright in their seats. Roswell International Air Center.

Now that was a game changer. Simon's office was so quiet you could hear Nick's hangover buzzing around in his head. All three looked at each other and neither had to say a word. They knew. This is what they were supposed to find.

Outside the glassed in office the other staff and management of the project were on about their daily routines. Neon ceiling lights buzzed on as they did every day. Keyboards clicked away as analysts and programmers alike filed their litany of information into the project database. Only the smell of coffee brewing in the cafeteria changed the typically dry fragrant less atmosphere of a government facility at work. If anyone had of looked up from their mundane endeavors they would have observed three ashen faced wraiths staring back at them from the other side of the boss's office. One would assume that all three had finally lost their minds over the absurdity of what they had been tasked to do and where now hopelessly lost in space, locked in an office together for all time.

In fact all three had thought the same thing at the same time with the same reaction. Someone in the office was not who they said they were and could even be the very thing that the project was set on destroying. All three had turned to the glass to look at the field of cubicles, each possibly containing an alien infiltrator.

ROAD TRIP

No one in Simon's office spoke for a good three minutes. Nick finally broke the ice.

"So, ok we know that someone hacked the data and sent a message a ten year old could have found. Then we get this cryptic image of a triangle shape something apparently lodged in the ground just outside the perimeter of the Roswell air field, which I for one, think is to damn big to be what we are all thinking it is. I mean seriously how the hell could you get something that big from the middle of the desert where there isn't a stick to play hide and seek behind and bury it in a populated area let alone the airport? But most of all how could anyone think that you could keep it hidden?"

"Road trip." Simon said.

"What?"

"Road trip. You know, we take the company jet down there and check it out."

Kim's eyes were as big as paper plates.

"I can't just take off, I have a schedule to follow and besides it would look pretty damn suspicious if all three of us take off together to Roswell New Mexico don't you think"

Simon thought she had a point, albeit a poor one. He could sense that she was more than a little un-nerved at the prospect of their actually being a real alien presence on earth. Even if the project she had been working on for almost a year had a mandate that specifically targeted aliens.

"Look we're too close to launch date and we don't have enough time to sit around and come up with a game plan to flush out our little bug in the office, so let's just come up with some flimsy reason to go down there, take a look around and find out what the fuck is going on."

Simon knew he wasn't going to get much of an argument from Nick. Nick was looking like he might need a place to pass out or at least have one more good hurl into a metal waste basket before he was all done.

"I agree with Nick, I did quick calculations on the triangle and it would be approximately 600 meters from tip to stern and just over that on the hypotenuse. He's right, that's a damn big piece of whatever to just bury in an airport no matter how you look at it."

Kim was getting a shade gray in the face too. "Ok, you stay Kim and see if you can run some geek software thing to find out who changed the data. Nick and I will ride down to New Mexico and have a look around. Ok Nick?"

Nick had passed out on the sofa in Simon's office. Just as well, Simon thought, he smelled like he had been at a frat party and had fallen asleep in the urinal.

ROSWELL NEW MEXICO

It wasn't hard for Simon to get the jet. It was really the first time in months that the project had required him to use the thing and since the brass had given him carte blanche to use whatever equipment he needed whenever he needed; it was easy to convince the board that they were going to Roswell to reconnoiter a blast hole.

If the boys in DC had any idea that they were dropping in on Roswell for any other reason than to check for a blast site, they didn't say a word. Actually Simon had slid the paper work for their little exploratory jaunt in amongst a bunch of other paper work and it had been signed off on without a second look.

The hardest part of the next couple of hours for Simon was getting Nick to rally. After a couple of black coffees laced with Grande Marnier and a steak sandwich in the bar upstairs in the hotel, Nick had come around somewhat so Simon grabbed a cab outside the front door and headed for the private hangar that the project kept at Ronald Reagan National. Since the airport hosted a shorter than most runway, it catered to a greater number of small jets and private airlines. That allowed the duo to arrive and board very inconspicuously. Not that Simon thought anyone would be watching anyway.

The trip to Reagan National was uneventful. Nick barely spoke two words except to grunt at whatever Simon threw at him in the way of conversation. To be honest, Simon didn't want to talk about where they were going, even in front of a cabby. Best that neither of them talked too much, which wasn't much of an effort for Nick?

The jet sat ready and waiting. Their paper work had been forwarded on to the check in at the private wing at Reagan. Neither Nick nor Simon thought that their little side trip would take more than 24 hours.

Once aboard both Simon and Nick felt a little more comfortable. The last couple of hours had been like every bad spy movie they had ever seen.

Take off was smooth and once in the air Nick finally got rid of his silent act.

"Remind me how much I hate Tequila next time someone proposes it as a stimulant."

"Fuck that" Simon laughed. "Your twenty five years younger than me and I still got to hold your head up so you don't puke on your shoes."

Nick looked back at Simon with blood shot eyes that in any other situation would have looked demonic but Simon knew he was still shaking out the cobwebs.

"So what do you think we should do once we get to Roswell?" Simon asked.

He still had no idea what they were looking for. After all, creeping around a secured government area of the airport was a bit risky even if they were essentially the government.

"I mean do you really think that something as outrageous as a giant alien craft is buried just outside the main runways of the Roswell International Airport? Shit man, it feeds every nut job conspiracy theory that ever existed, not to mention the sheer size of the thing. How the hell could you possibly hide something like that in plain sight?"

"Listen, people have been making big things disappear since Harry Houdini made an elephant disappear on a New York stage in 1918. The only difference here is the size of it. It's not so much can it be done as how did they do it. Houdini's trick remained a secret for almost 90 years. Let's face it; there might not be anything there when we get there. It could all be a ruse to keep us away from the project. Did you think of that? But if there is something buried under the ground at Roswell International Airport, you can be damn sure who ever hid it there isn't going to let us just walk up and dig a hole and go looking for it."

Up until that remark Simon had been happy just to be out of the shop. The invasion deadline was approaching quick and since the last test blast had been successful there wasn't much to do but manage the ongoing digging of blast wells around the continent and abroad. He was actually feeling a bit like Sherlock Holmes, confident that his ability to reason, backed with a scientific background would lead him successfully to the conclusion of their little mystery. He really hadn't factored in that there might be some forcible reaction to their investigation.

That was as far as that thought got as he suddenly became overcome by the vilest of stenches. It was unlike anything that he had experienced outside of his own fart vault (his bedroom back in Detroit). It was as if the hounds of hell had combined all their bad breath after a day of eating their own stools and blew him a kiss.

Since there was only he and Nick in the cabin of the plane, and he was pretty dam sure that he was still alive, the only conclusion could be that Nick had farted. An SBD, the worst kind, Silent But Deadly. This was starting out to be the longest five hours of his life.

Fortunately for Simon, Nick's unfortunate flatulence was a onetime killer. The rest of the flight consisted of theories. What? How? What if? Eventually Simon got an idea.

"Since we have access to all the government files, let's do a little search of the Roswell airport blueprints and see if there is anything that looks a bit hinky. Specifically anything that might hint at underground access to the fields on either side of the Will Rogers road.

Both agreed that they would do exactly that as soon as the plane landed.

The afternoon was getting on as the two conspirators flew west. The late day sun shone golden through the windows of the cabin and both men nodded on and off as they succumbed to the effects of the late night and the days revelations.

The landing at Roswell was so soft that neither Nick nor Simon awoke from their naps until the pilot shook them awake.

The sun was below the horizon but there was still enough light to find their way to the hangar that the jet had pulled up to. The crappy wooden door and corrugated steel siding belayed the bright warm interior that smelled of freshly brewed coffee and jet fuel.

The two were met by a heavy set man in his forties carrying an armload of rolled up, what looked to be, rolls of architectural drawings.

"Name's Simpson, your girl in DC phoned a couple of hours ago and said you might have use of the airport blueprints. These days this shit is usually kept under lock and key but I've always kept a dupe set for myself. I do most of the maintenance and problem sourcing for all the out buildings here. If I had to go looking for security every time I needed a blueprint or a sat map for the place nothing would get done."

Simon and Nick looked at one another.

"What was the girls' name?" Simon inquired. "I think she said it was Kim, said it had something to do with National Security. She said you two would show credentials when you got here. Anyway, here's the lot. If you got some kind of ID on ya it would be good. Most of these buildings are so far from the main terminal if you were planning to blow one of em up you would be doing us a favor. At least you would be doing me a favor. Then I wouldn't have to maintain the damn thing. You're not going to blow any shit up are you?"

Nick reached under his jacket and pulled out his project ID card that hung from everyone's neck back in DC. While not looking much like any FBI or CIA badge it obviously looked official enough for Simpson as he just grunted and headed for a door in the sidewall of the big hangar.

"Coffee in the office if you need one, phones in there too. Let me know if you need anything else. Just hit Simpson on the speed dial.

Simon and Nick just looked at one another and burst out laughing.

"Shit, if we were trying to blow something up it would be pretty easy around here"

They were still chucking to themselves as they began to roll out the blue prints of the airport and the surrounding out buildings. Specifically they wanted to focus on the east side of the outer fence.

They had brought a copy of the satellite photo that Kim had discovered and after laying it out along side of the blueprints the first thing they noticed was that the bottom of the triangle anomaly that they had discovered in the sat photo was defined by a road called, Will Rogers Road. Between that and the airport was the drag racing track with a number of corrugated out buildings. They could see that from where they stood, just off the main runway 21, they could almost walk to Will Rodgers Road and investigate the area. It didn't look like there was a single fence between them and the object of their investigation.

"That's just too fucking convenient." Simon said.

"You're right about that, but look here." Nick pointed to the drag track directly adjacent to the field they were interested in.

"These buildings here are pretty old looking. They're also big enough to house or hide machinery or anything you want for that matter. Could be we could start there and see what's what."

"I think your right about that but let's focus on this one here. It looks like there is a trailer attached to the building. That's a bit odd unless you have someone living on site full time."

Simon had pointed to the building closest to their immediate position and Nick had agreed.

"We just need some transportation. I don't feel like walking over there in the dark especially without some kind of protection."

Nick reached under his coat and pulled out a snubbie Cobra handgun.

"We have some protection."

"Where the hell did you get that" Simon wasn't shocked as much as interested.

"Used to be my dad's. I left my service weapon in the top drawer of my desk at the office. If anyone comes snooping it will look like our trip wasn't important enough to warrant a gun."

"Ok then, let's go see if Simpson can get us hooked up with some wheels and we can get this checked out.

THE CORE

It wasn't too hard to find Simpson. Nick and Simon had crossed the hangar from where they had laid out the plans to the where they had seen Simpson enter the office. They pulled open the door and found him asleep at the only desk in the place, head back and legs up on the open first drawer.

Nick gave the door a little extra shove to announce their presence and the ensuing bang did wake the sleeping maintenance man but just barely.

"What the?" It was clear there were still a few cobwebs to be cleared.

"Hey there Simpson, where do you think we could get some wheels around here without having to get permission or renting one?"

Simon was using his best authoritative voice but didn't think it really mattered. He was pretty sure the handy man was the right guy to ask.

"Well depends on what you have in mind but if you're not looking for speed you can take the old golf cart I use to get around the hangars. Its right out front and the keys in it. If anybody stops you just tell them to call me."

"Thanks." Nick said. "We'll bring it back in one piece."

As they turned to leave Simpson was re-establishing his position in the chair. It really looked like he didn't give a shit one way or the other.

The front door to the hangar was on the opposite side of the office. Outside the golf cart was right where Simpson had said. Both men sat in the cart for a moment without turning it on. Simon spoke first.

"You know, I don't have much experience with covert goings on but I do know when someone is yanking my chain. Either this guy is the best actor in the entire world and we are being set up or there is just really nothing here and there is nothing to hide."

"I was thinking the same thing but with one variation. It would be good to see when certain people were hired here. I'd like to see the correlation between the UFO sighting in the area, specifically the crash sighting and when people in certain positions got the call. It might not be so much as they are in on it as they just might not know. Simpson seems like a regular Joe but maybe he's a particularly gullible Joe and can't or won't see past the end of his broom or the end of his job. See no, speak no sorta thing."

Nick had a point Simon thought, but they had come this far and they had a pretty good point of investigation so they turned on the cart and headed out the back of the hangar area and onto Will Rogers Road south.

The golf cart had been fitted with headlamps. Probably so the little cart could be seen while darting amongst the huge hangars in the dark.

Will Rodgers Road wasn't hard to find. It was a well-kept main artery to the drag racing track that bisected the racetrack and the field that they were interested in. It was another ten minutes to the drag strip itself but it was well marked and the main gate stood open.

"Too easy I'm thinking. I keep getting the feeling that we are being led right down the garden path."

"Like I said Simon, either real smart or just don't know."

Either way they drove right through the front gate and pulled up to the corrugated building where they had seen the trailer parked out back.

The night was dark but warm, the cool wind generated from the carts forward momentum had kept them comfortable.

Once they stopped the proximity of the metal building, still cooling in the early evening breeze, brought on an instant sweat. They crossed the short distance to the front door and peered in the window. The interior was empty, clean really. Too clean for a building of its size and relationship to the drag strip. An attempt to turn the knob proved the door to be locked so they headed to the back along the paved surface of the parking lot that surrounded the building on three sides.

The heat of the day still made the asphalt feel soft and malleable, as if every step sunk into the pavement just a little. You could smell the tar melting underfoot.

The back of the building was not paved and resembled an un-kept field. Tall weeds surrounded the patch of dirt that contained the ramshackle trailer. The trailer itself wasn't actually attached to the shed but there was evidence that there had been quite a bit of foot traffic between it and the back door of the building buy the clean path that had been worn through the surrounding weed bed.

"I think we should see if we can get into the hangar first. The trailer looks like it might have someone in it. I'd rather not have to explain ourselves or run into any security at this point if we don't have to." Simon whispered to Nick.

"Give the door a shot." Nick urged.

The nob turned without any effort, as if it had been in use for some time. The door itself opened, thankfully without a creak and both men entered the stifling heat of the hangars interior.

The hangar was large, probably half the size of a football field and unlit. Simon and Nick took a few seconds for their eyes to acclimatize to the dark interior. Lit only by the ambient light of the half-moon and a few far placed light posts on the front side of the building there was just enough elimination to see that the place was clean. Real clean. Like to the point of never been used. The corrugated tin walls and roof had been painted a marine gray and the cement floor was polished to a high gloss. The rough exterior belayed the squeaky clean inside to the point of ridiculous.

"What do they do in here? Nick whispered. Surgery?"

They stepped through the door way and into the sterile interior.

As soon as their feet hit the concrete floor both men nearly jumped out of their skins. There was a palpable hum associated with the place. Not a sound, but a vibration that came from below. It could have been just in the floor but was more like it took over the entire volume of the space inside the building. It wasn't unlike one of those vibrating beds that you could get in a cheap hotel in Vegas. You popped a quarter into the slot in the headboard and the bed vibrated for a few minutes. Just like that, only a higher frequency more intense and definitely unnerving.

"What the fuck do you think that could be?" Simon's voice had a bit of vibrato in it, like driving down a rickety country road.

"Don't know." Nick replied. "But you can be damn sure it ain't normal and this far out from the airport it has nothing to do with runway light generators or anything else to do with that. It's too damn big."

"How come we didn't feel it on the way in?"

"Might be something in the concrete, maybe if it's re-enforced with rebar or just the cement pad itself that is picking up the frequency."

"Well whatever it is it's making me want to puke."

Both Nick and Simon got outside in time to refrain from up-chucking their stomach contents. Nick thought that was a good thing since his abs had already taken a beating from the hurl fest earlier in the day.

"That was crazy, what the hell do you think is causing that?"

"Never felt anything like that before so can't really guess but I think we should have a look at this trailer. Maybe it has something to do with it."

The trailer like the back door was unlocked which made Simon think that again, it was just too easy, someone was leading them on.

Inside the trailer the heat was intense. So was the smell. It was obvious no one lived in the thing. Cupboards hung from rusting hinges, Styrofoam seats in the kitchen nook and bed were yellowed with age and rotting. The carpet was so degenerated that Simon thought it was lucky he wasn't wearing sandals.

With the most trepidation he had felt all night Simon pulled open the door to the bathroom expecting to be totally grossed out. Hoping he would not find an ancient remnant of some goliath bowel movement he peered in.

As his eyes adjusted to the dimly lit alcove he was met with the second surprise of the night. The bathroom was as clean as the building they had just left. The walls wrapped in stainless steel, the fixtures modern and clean.

Now for the big test, Simon thought, as he reached for the toilet lid.

His first attempt to flip it up, left him cursing and nursing his fingernail where the edge of the seat had pulled it away from the quick. The next attempt he made sure to keep his nails hidden as he reefed on the sides to try and pry the lid from the seat.

His grunting exercise brought Nick to the washroom.

"What's all the fuss boss, you need some help to take a dump."

"Very funny, take a look at this and see if it feels like a joke to you. I can't get the damn lid up." Nick peered into the little washroom and had to admit. It was weird looking. Simon stepped back and Nick forced his bulk into the tiny space. His efforts at raising the seat met with the same dismal results as Simons and after a couple of tries Nick gave up.

"Curiouser and curiouser. Simon said. This has to be something more than just a very odd bathroom in a rundown trailer in the middle of nowhere at the airport in Roswell."

"Well when you say it like that, it doesn't sound that odd."

The laugh in Nick's voice did nothing to remove the level of anxiety that Simon was beginning to feel.

"Did you check to see if any of the taps or the toilet was working?" Nick asked, trying to sound a bit more serious.

"Shit, I was too busy trying to get the seat up. I guess I was expecting some giant turd to come flying out.

Simon reached over and tried to flush the toilet.

"Nothing, this is just too weird looking to not have some other purpose."

"I agree." Nick said.

"Try the taps."

Nick gave the hot and the cold water taps a healthy twist.

"Those feel like their welded on."

The mirror over the sink was obviously of the same vintage as the rest of the place. The center was still able to form an image but the sides had begun to lose their mercury and had made inroads toward the center like the trails left in the sand of an ant farm.

Nick leaned in to take a look at himself, not from vanity but from habit.

As he rested both hands on the edge of the small basin his right hand encountered a grooved indentation in the edge.

Without thinking Nick just pushed it in.

A whoosh of warm air exploded in their faces as the bathroom enclosure and everything in it dropped like a carnival thrill ride.

The drop only lasted about 20 seconds but for all of that time Simon and Nick had been held prisoner against the ceiling of the capsule, speechless and unable to move from the force of the fall. Both their ears had popped violently before they came to an abrupt stop, Simon landing heavily on Nick and thankful he had.

"What the fuck was that?" Simon exclaimed, out of breath. Even though he had landed on Nick the impact on landing had knocked some of the air out of his lungs.

"I'd say that was about 200 feet judging by the compression pop my ears just got." Nick seemed unfazed by the abrupt departure from the shack behind the hangar. Both were still entangled on the floor of the tiny capsule but as they unraveled themselves it was obvious that they had come down some kind of elevator shaft and where once the bathroom door had lead out into the trash filled trailer, there was now no door at all, just open access to a dimly lit cavern beyond the sill.

"We could be in some shit here Nick. Nobody goes to this much trouble to hide an elevator like that if they wanted a couple of snoops to just fall right in. Not only that, you don't dig a hole that big underground unless you got some serious mining equipment and a shit load of men to dig it out."

Nick had to agree. The question was, what's the next move? Do they take a leap and move forward or just push the little button back in on the side of the vanity and see if the thing goes back up?

It was odd. Even though the cavern was partially lit it wasn't damp or musty. The slight breeze that passed by their ears on its way up the elevator shaft was warm and friendly almost. Neither one felt as if they were threatened or that there was anything ominous about the place.

"Let's give it a shot." Simon's curiosity had gotten the better of him. He had never expected anything as crazy as this when he work up this morning but had just been kicking his ass not that long ago about missed opportunity and the lack of excitement in his life. Why the hell was he hesitating?

With that Simon stepped out of there their shitty little sanctuary onto the floor of the open room.

To his surprise just like the floor in the hangar above there was an instant sense of the jitters. Almost as if a very low electrical current was being passed through his body. That and the funny vibrato in his voice when he spoke.

"It's just like up top in the hangar but without the sick feeling." He hollered back at Nick.

Why he was talking so loud he didn't really know but Nick, who had cautiously followed him through the hole, looked like he felt the same thing. He had also taken out the gun that until then he had kept tucked into the back of his pants.

The vastness of the cave made the revolver in Nicks had look even smaller than it was.

"I got a feeling that won't be of much use. This is huge. There's probably a rocket launcher in here somewhere."

It didn't look like it mattered to Nick; he was keeping the gun out anyway.

"Let's see if there is an end to this hole."

Their eyes had become accustomed to the dull light and they could see a few yards ahead without too much trouble. Picking a direction was going to be hard because except for the door that led to the bathroom elevator the rest seemed endless.

"What are you thinking?" Simon queried.

Nick pondered a moment. "Well it's a crap shoot I think but let's just move forward in a straight line from the door way and see if we get anywhere in a couple of minutes." It wasn't much of a plan but what the hell Simon thought, got to do something?

A CONSPIRATORS DREAM

The floor of the cavern, at least what Simon could see of it, looked to be as clean and pristine as the one in the hangar. They could tell it was made up of tons and tons of concrete even in the little distance they had traveled after leaving the doorway. Still he had a feeling of wellbeing along with the constant thrum of the current still niggling at his innards. Nothing had jumped out of the dark to strangle them or rip their hearts out and it did look like there was a tiny slit of light up ahead.

It felt like forever to reach the line of light. In fact it was only three minutes. Still a long three minutes staring into the darkness wondering where the hell they were.

The light turned out to be a line of filament that was imbedded in the floor just short of what appeared to be a huge steel wall.

As they came up to the illuminated strip the ceiling gave way to an endless open space above their heads cathedral shaped and rising into the darkness above them. The wall in front arced away on either side curving away in an endless line of steel into the darkness. As the two men stared up at the huge expanse above their heads both inadvertently stepped over the glowing line in the floor. The boom that erupted directly in front of them almost knocked them off their feet as a door so big you could have moved a 20 story building though it if the thing was on wheels, opened before them.

The rush of air that followed the thunderous opening was not unpleasant and smelled faintly of the tropics. More like suntan lotion and brine Simon thought, still gaping up at the vastness of the doors.

"What the hell is this place?" He wondered aloud.

Nick didn't have any words. He was in a bit of shock and couldn't quite find his voice.

Simon on the other hand was still feeling the rush of adrenalin the door opening had started and he decided to just go with it. He hoped the extra excitement wouldn't end in a stroke and on that note he just walked into the void ahead.

The space was now lit with the same luminous light that they had seen in the floor and while it did give some sense of time and space it still was dim enough to mask the surroundings. There was an idea of outlines in the wall and both men followed them to the right, the floor beneath their feet no longer concrete but some type of carbon steel material. Simon abruptly stopped.

"Hey, do you feel that?" Nick just stared at him.

"The buzzing is gone."

Nick started to pat himself down like he was looking for a pack of smokes.

"Oh, yea, it's almost like you had a weird massage of some kind. My legs still feel a bit rubbery and tingly but your right. It's completely gone.

Simon thought it was probably the change of floor material that had quelled the crazy electrical feeling.

They resumed their walk keeping the curvature of the wall to their right. As they progressed they turned into a tunnel, almost like a service conduit in a large building only bigger. Now the walls were definitely smoother than they had been on the other side of the big door and they were crisscrossed with a labyrinth of imbedded ridges that you could clearly make out as some type of electrical and possibly venting tubes. The original buzz that they had left behind on the other side of the door now emanated from the walls. Not quit as high a pitch as before but a definite droning like the rumblings of the huge engines that drive an aircraft carrier. There was a cyclical rise and fall to the sound giving it an essence of huge power.

As they walked neither said a word to one another. The corridor remained constant in height and width as they cautiously moved forward but the thrumming from the walls had continued to gain strength. Not so much in volume but in body. They knew that whatever was making the place hum wasn't too far up ahead.

When they had been following their arched hallway for about ten minutes it abruptly came to an end. It didn't just come to a wall but opened onto an enormous, cavernous space, possibly as long as two football fields and easily one wide, the ceiling height was indeterminate as it rose into the darkness.

Centered and seemingly imbedded in the floor of the area, a gigantic engine, or what was some science fiction version of an engine. Its outer surface area resembled a couple of hundred giant twin cylinder heads like those of a V twin Viago motor cycle lined up one after the other for the length of the enclosure. A warm mat finish colored sky blue covered some of the outer flanges, the ones on the right of the V moving clockwise with the counter clockwise spin of its twin on the left.

Closer to the floor semi-circle plates of gold covered the bottom part of the mechanism, not holding it in place but changing position with each rhythmic cycle of the machine. Possibly some type of counterbalance. Above the last 50 or so of the V twins a rotating bundle of light, aqua marine and light blue like the color of a Caribbean sea as the sun shines through the ripples, swirled, tunnel like but round at the same time. Huge arcs of yellow merged with other outward flowing streams, billowing solar flares dissipating into thin air as the next stream of light followed it outward from the ball. There was no sound of electricity or static charge just the slowly turning and rolling mass.

To the front or at least what Simon assumed was the front a structure that gleamed like polished steel rose up at least six stories high. It was shaped like an ancient jousting helm, curved forward and face like, arching out to a point about midway down and supported by a middle a structure that was urn shaped and transparent. Huge venting plates in the lower half of the mask ran parallel to the floor and moved outward and inward as if breathing life into the huge engine in front of it. Inside the urn an obvious circular stair structure wound its way up to the upper face of the mask where an observation area back lit with yellow light peered out onto the rows of V twins and up into the ball of blue light.

It was a long way away but Simon could swear he saw some movement behind the glassed in the observation deck.

That slightest of movements, so small and so far away was human in its way and it woke Simon from his revelry.

"Are you seeing what I think I'm seeing?" he asked Nick.

"I think I peed a little." Nick replied.

Simon couldn't help it. He burst out laughing. His hilarity was short lived however as there was suddenly someone speaking to him. Not an ambient voice but inside his head.

He naturally looked around for the body that went with it and he noticed Nick doing the exact same thing. It sounded like he had headphones on and the voice was right inside his head.

"Gentlemen," the voice said, "please continue to follow the corridor to your right. It is a bit of a walk but we don't usually use that end of the core for anything other than the occasional visit from our guards."

This time it was Simons turn to pee a little.

"Who is this?" his voice louder than usual just like if you were wearing headphones and were trying to talk over whatever you were listening to.

"Please just follow the corridor and we will try to make sure you don't pee any more than you have too."

If Simon didn't know better he would think someone was really yanking his chain but unless this was some incredible dream or he had been hypnotized and drugged at the same time he wasn't going to miss this either way. No matter what the outcome he was off down the corridor with Nick silently behind.

The trek to the other end of whatever it was that they were trudging around in was in fact considerably longer that Simon would have guessed. A full eight minutes had passed and it still looked like they had some walking to do.

Five minutes later Simon could see what he assumed was the, in head commentator, standing at the bottom of what he was calling the observation deck.

"Hey, do you see that guy standing there?" Nick asked.

"Yea, I was just thinking he was the guy talking inside my head."

Nick seemed surprised. "You heard that too? I thought I was hallucinating or something."

"Yea, I heard it too. You might be right though, we could be hallucinating."

They had come within a few feet of the person but came up short as both men realized at the same time that it wasn't a person. Not really. It was more of a person-like person. The general shape was human but the skin, it had the color of high end carbon fiber yet moved and flowed like skin when the entity began to speak.

'Welcome." It said to Simon and Nick.

The long brown hair pulled straight back from the forehead gave the head a majestic appearance. The body was clothed in modern pant and shirt with the typical footwear one would find in any big city departments store.

The extended hand accompanied by the typical Midwest welcome took both men by surprise.

Simon reached out to take the proffered appendage before he even realized he was doing it.

The grip was firm and welcoming and felt as normal as any hand shake anywhere in the world. The one difference was that the feel belayed the reality.

Though the skin of the greeter felt human, it sure didn't look human.

The same polished look of carbon fiber was evident on the hands as well as the face.

Simon could actually say that it was a face now. As he moved to shake the greeters hand he closed the gap between them. He could clearly make out that the body had a very human looking face attached to it. Eyes, nose and ears were in similar locations. There did look to be some kind of vented opening near the hairline but the only light in the place was coming from the thrumming giant ball of plasma turning away over the V twins of the engine and some that shone down from the observation deck, so he couldn't be completely sure.

"You must have a million questions and you are probably getting a bit tired. It would seem that the electromagnetic field set up by our jailers has that effect on humans. Funny, really when you think of it. Something as simple as a magnet and an electrical current could tame even the huge power generated by our Coronial Sling Systems"

The lips were moving but the voice was still inside Simons head. Just like it had been the first time. He gave it a shake and then tried to hold his nose while blowing air into his nasal passages, a trick often used by divers to level the air pressure in their ears.

"That won't help." The voice said. "I am talking to you inside your head because my natural form of speech would not be comprehensible to you. I am moving my lips to form the words as you would see anyone do but it is because I memorized these movements from watching TV and to try and make it more comfortable for our guardians when I talk."

"So can you understand me when I talk then?" Simon asked.

"Yes, you can talk normally and I will understand you. I can speak a number of earth dialects. I have had some time on my hands since 1947."

I knew it, Simon thought, fucking government has kept this secret since the crash in 47.

"Exactly right Simon, except for the fucking part", the voice inside Simons head responded.

"Did I say that out loud?" Simon looked bewildered.

"No," the carbon man replied, "I can also read your thoughts. One of the reasons I have been kept here so long. Your Government is all about the mind reading thing."

Simons mind was whirling, as probably was Nicks. Nick had been rooted to the spot since they had passed through the door into the engine chamber.

"Hey," Nick blurted out. "It's almost midnight. We gotta get our asses back before someone gets suspicious."

Nicks outburst gave Simon a start but he had to agree. It was enough that they had commandeered the jet to go on this adventure but it was going to be hard to explain where they had disappeared too for 6 hours while they were just out walking around if the brass back home started asking questions.

"I see your dilemma, let me give you the quick version and then I will send you on your way."

"In 1947 we came to earth in a prototype vehicle that you are standing in now. As you look at the drive force before here you might think that that trip would have been fairly quick. Not so. Our origin is a star many light years behind the star Tau Sagittarii in the Chi Sagittarii star Group. We knew from advanced telescopic detective work that your planet also held life. The only other we had found in our solar system. We were curious and with the new technology of the Coronial Sling System we were able to make the distance.

After many months of dodging asteroid belts and space dust storms we arrived in the atmosphere of your world. It was a great deal like our own, water based plant life creating a breathable atmosphere and over millennia produced a culture very similar to ours. The difference is that our atmosphere is 30 times heavier than the one that exists on earth. So over millions of years we developed this form of exoskeleton that you keep refereeing to as carbon fiber. In that you would not be far wrong but we found a way to evolve our own outer skin to take on the complexity of your epidermis so though it appears carbon like it has the same pliable properties of human skin.

So, on to the real reason you are here. We explored your world under the cover of darkness and the cover of weather without detection, even though our craft was huge in comparison to anything earth had in the 40s. Unfortunately until that night in 1947, just the other side of the town we are under now, we had successfully went our way without incident. That night we were hiding in thick low cloud using our instruments to observe the comings and goings of earth. It was a mistake to not take into consideration the dryness of the desert air here which mixed with the damp cloud cover created a huge electromagnetic burst witch temporarily interrupted our systems. We could not recover control in time to keep from crashing so we chose a section of desert that was uninhabited and let the craft go, confident that it would only take a short time to repair. Little did we realize that you humans would be so quick to discover us in this isolated place. Another unlucky thing for us was once found out your army used electro magnets to anchor our ship until they could figure out what it was and what to do with us.

I won't bore you with the details of how we ended up here under the Roswell Municipal Airport but let's just say we still haven't figured out to this day how to break the elector magnet hold and free ourselves. It should be such a simple thing but something in our propulsion rhythm just doesn't like the magnets. This whole thing, including you two, comes down to your WOW signal. Yes, I can see by the look on your face, you're wondering how I know about that. Look, your being fooled by those in charge. They told you that the WOW signal was from outer space and that aliens were coming to take over earth. They probably told you that there was a blatant threat in the message right?

Both Simon and Nick just looked at one another and nodded.

Well that is not exactly the truth. The truth is that my people are coming to earth, not in anger but to try and get us back. Your marines have a motto. "No man left behind." Well we have a similar motto, it's just that it has taken a long time for our people to rebuild a similar stellar travel machine. They are not coming in anger. That is just a fable made up by your military so they can continue to get funding for projects such as yours. They would make everyone believe that your world was in danger so they can move forward their war agendas and make money from whatever the result.

My friends are coming to get me and they will not expect some hideous onslaught of germ warfare or ballistic welcome wagons. You would in fact be committing murder if you go forward with your current project.

Simon was still in disbelief over the entity that he was discoursing with and the incredible tale he had just been told.

Nick, having not said more than a couple of words for almost half an hour finally found his tough.

"That's a lot to take in, ah mister, what do I call you?"

"Wayne" the carbon man said.

Both men burst out laughing.

"How the hell did you get a name like Wayne?" Nick asked.

"I'm glad you find humor in this name." Wayne said. "I was named after one of you famous movie stars, John Wayne. I have my real name but it would not be a word you could pronounce."

"Sorry about that, it's just that you don't look like a Wayne. Really a long way from it." Nick nodded in agreement.

"So how did you know we were coming here and how could you have manipulated us to this point."

Wayne turned to Nick and for the first time Simon could see that they were both almost the same size. Nick was a pretty big boy by any sense but Wayne was possibly a half a head taller and quite a bit broader in the shoulders.

"Well that's the fun part. Over the years your people have found it interesting to try and create a hybrid between my people and yours. No physical mating, our anatomy and seminal biological structure would not have been good for a human woman. Too much heavy metal. But they did manage to artificially create a number of cross bred children and gave them to us to raise until they felt it time to remove them and try to conform them to human ideals. I think they had delusions of super humans. Too bad they didn't realize that our culture has no greater physical attributes that yours. We have no greater mental ability than yours. We might look different but it is only because our culture is a few thousand years older than yours that we have developed the technology for galactic space travel. The only thing that I could say is unusual is how we can communicate. With you I can hear you and talk to you inside your head as long as long as you are not too far away. I can even communicate with humans at some distance outside this prison if I choose to. The further away the more scrambled the communication becomes until I can't hear anything. With our children I can communicate quite decently at good distance. That is something your government was hoping to exploit. Can you imagine if they had a group of individuals who could tell you what everyone in the room was thinking? Imagine the control you would have over your enemies. We managed to keep the transference of thought a secret.

When we realized what their agenda really was we pre-taught some of our youth in areas that we thought might help our cause in the future. One of those children works in your secret basement complex next to the Mayflower Hotel in Washington DC. He set you on this path so we could talk. You must have known that there was more to your agenda than just saving the earth form alien invaders. Those are stories made up by your government and imaginative screen writers. Your whole idea of who I am and what my culture is has been warped by popular science and government cover ups. How else do you think something as big as this craft could be kept buried in an airfield in such a notorious town without anyone questioning the odd shape in the ground and the abandoned yet immaculately kept buildings surrounding it?"

He had a point but it was all so surreal. Simon could barely grasp the fact that he was actually talking to a real live alien. He felt no threat, no animosity, truly his only thought was, how the hell we are going to get out of here.

Nick said what was really on both their minds.

"So what is it you expect us to do?"

"I would hope that now, knowing the truth, you would try to find a way to resolve the issue. Notwithstanding the fact that we have been held captive here for so long against our will but to find a way to halt your solution to exterminate our comrades who are only trying to save us. Something you would do yourselves in the same situation."

"So how do we know you are telling us the truth" Nick asked.

A fair question Simon thought.

"Really, you wouldn't have to look very hard to find the truth. Get Kim to look into some of the funding documents and the back grounds of your circle of friends. She has the access to dig deeper than just superficial documentation. It's there. Follow the money.

Simon was surprised at how much information this Wayne had. He knew the names of those in his innermost office. Still he wasn't about to take this things word for it, even if they were standing in a gigantic engine room, the likes he could only have thought possible in a Hollywood movie.

"So, convince us that what you say is true." He said.

"It is time for you to go." Was Wayne's reply, "I will send you proof."

The warehouse floor was humming like an electric toothbrush. Simon became aware of his surroundings likely the same time as Nick. Both men spun in a circle, taking in the corrugated steel walls of the building they had just entered or felt like they just entered.

Where had the huge alien engine room gone and where was their tour guide and alien confidant Wayne?

Could the strange vibration in the floor have scrambled their brains, maybe hypnotized them somehow.

The only thing that fit was that when Simon took a look at his watch over six hours had elapsed since they had originally entered the building.

"Let's get the hell out of here." Nick seemed a bit frantic and Simon was only too happy to oblige.

The cool desert air outside calmed their nerves somewhat but not enough that Nicks voice didn't have a bit of a hitch in it when he asked Simon.

"Did you see what I saw or was that some kind of a mind blowing brain fuck thing?"

Simon wasn't sure what a brain fuck thing was but if Nick meant meeting an alien on board his buried space craft and having a conversation about human conspiracy to hide said space craft and the fact that they were there and more were coming, than yes, he saw it too.

The questions were, should they believe it, who would believe them and what should they do about it?

Now outside the steel building with its vibrating floor, the whole thing was like a weird trip. Could they possibly have ingested some kind of a time delayed hallucinogen while on the plane? Simon wasn't sure about anything right at this point but he did know one thing. He knew how the good old boys in the office liked to have their wars and ammo too. They would stop at nothing to keep an arms contract or whatever military scenario would continue to bring them an income. It wouldn't surprise him in the least if this whole thing came down to a couple of Colonels trying to hedge their retirement funds.

One thing for sure, they had to get their asses back to the office and see if Kim had come up with anything else. They also had to find out who might in fact be an alien intruder in the office. Just the thought of an actual being from outer space having access to the labs seemed ludacris.

When Simon and Nick arrived back at the hangar they were both still in a state of disbelief. It was still dark enough outside that they thought their little adventure would likely go unnoticed and if they had any worries that Simpson would have questions or concerns they needn't have, he was still fast asleep at his desk.

"Where do I get a job like that?" Nick asked.

"Let's just get the hell out of here before he wakes up." Simon replied.

The jet was dark and quiet when the two men boarded. They found the pilot fast asleep splayed out over one of the couches in the luxury cabin.

Nick hit the button to raise the gangway and the whirring of the motors woke him. "Let's go home."

"Aye Aye." The Captain replied as he jumped to the cockpit and started flipping switches.

Simon and Nick settled in to the plush leather seats of the Lear but not before pouring a couple good stiff drinks. They were going to have to figure out what their next steps were going to be before the plane landed in DC.
The three hour trip back to DC was filled with whispered conversation. As if the two men were in a library. They speculated on everything from whether the whole thing was a hallucination of some kind to who was responsible for such a huge cover up if it was real.

Nick had found his voice after having barely spoke more than a few sentences over the last twelve hours. Simon knew it was partly the severe hangover he had started the day with but the rest he put down to shock. He had to admit, he was a bit shocked himself. The more he thought about the six hours they had spent under the Roswell Airport the more it felt unbelievable.

"Something like that would cost millions a year don't you think" Nick's question brought Simon back from the land of make believe and aliens.

"Your right about that. Maybe that's what Wayne was talking about, remember? Follow the money, he said?

"Right," Nick responded, "that kinda dough would definitely leave a trail of some kind no matter how hard you tried to hide it"

"We'll get Kim to check that out when we get back. First things first, I got to get some sleep. Maybe when I wake up this will all be a dream or a joke or something."

That's exactly what I'm hoping too." Nick was relieved that Simon wasn't all that comfortable with their discovery either.

Touchdown in DC was much like it had been in Roswell. The only difference was the humidity. Washington was humid and Simon started sweating the minute they left the air-conditioned jet.

The pilot had phoned ahead to keep a car ready for them and they wasted little time jumping in the back.

Once they were off the airport grounds officially there was an audible exhale from both men. Simon had sat back and had his eyes closed when he felt a little tug on his sleeve. His eyes popped open and when he looked down Nick was sliding a piece of paper into his hand. The movement was rather secretive so Simon deduced that Nick was trying to keep the driver from seeing his actions.

Simon slid the paper into the pocket of his jacket and returned to his half dozing until they reached the hotel.

"Get some sleep Nick and let's do a debriefing in the morning."

"Right Boss." Nick replied, hoping that it sounded like just another day on the job.

When Simon got to his room he pulled the little crumpled up piece of paper that Nick had slid him in the limo and opened it up. *There will be ears everywhere*, it read. That was Nick's agent background talking. In the frenzy to get a viable launch vehicle ready and the search for the right virus to send into the atmosphere, Simon had forgotten that Nick was also a trained field agent. A good thing to remember if they were to start scrutinizing what they were doing and who's agenda they were really following.

His bed never felt so good, even though he hadn't been to his real home in a few months, his room at the Mayflower was comfortable and the bed was opulent. He loved the fact that there was maid service that changed the sheets and left fresh soap, shampoo and moisturizer every day after he left for the office. He was really going to miss this place when this whole thing was over.

Simon was asleep the second his head hit the pillow but nightmarish scenes of alien battles full of runny nosed carbon men with laser beams shooting out of their eyes and huge rotating orbs of light that burned everything in their path kept jolting him awake. No matter how hard he tried to think of something else the second he went back to sleep he was right back to where he left off when he woke up.

FOLLOW THE MONEY

He was awakened by the ringing of the phone on the night table beside his bed. The shrill twirling of the bell brought him to a fuzzy reality made only slightly better by the fact that he thought he finally had a couple of hours sleep without nightmares.

The phone call was Nick. "Hey, you back from the dead yet? You're late for work and Kim has been pestering the hell out of me for the last hour to tell her what happened in Roswell but I've been putting her off. I want to make sure you were here so it won't sound too unreal when we tell her."

"What time is it" Simon grunted into the phone.

"It's ten, take your time, no one's looking for you."

"Got it, be right over."

Simon turned the hot water on full. He needed the shock of heat to clear his head and the burn worked better for him than the cold. He could never figure out why people used cold water to shock themselves or others. Yea he got that the cold was a shocker but so was heat, and he would much rather be hot than cold. Probably those crappy lake effect winters in Detroit. The Great Lakes could really throw a blizzard at you and when the damp cold air off Lake St. Claire got in your bones, there was nothing for it but to huddle up in front of a fireplace somewhere with a big bottle of Jim Beam and drink until you were sweating. At least that was how he used to do it in the past. Lately he just stood under a really hot shower head until he couldn't take it anymore. It had the same effect on him anyway.

The office looked and felt like it did every other day. Even though Simon was really hoping that it would look different after his experience in Roswell, it was still just a boring office and labs, with boring lab techs and computer geeks going about their boring day trying to save the world through nuclear blasting and nanite technology. It sounded crazy when he thought about it that way but they were down to the crunch and now like every other time in his life, out poped the monkey. Just when he had the whole thing figured out, just when he was on the brink of accomplishing what he had set out to prove so many years ago, a twist. This time it was going to be different. He would get to the bottom of whatever was going on and he wasn't fucking around. This time he was gonna have that monkeys balls.

As he entered the common area of the basement lab Simon could see that Nick and Kim had already taken up residence in his office. Kim was facing his way and waved at him as he zigzagged through the labyrinth of cubicles to join them.

Judging by the empty coffee cups and the donut remnants it appeared that the two had been there for some time.

"Must be nice to just come waltzing in whenever you feel like it." The laughter in Nick's voice betrayed his faux hostility. It was also good to hear the confidence back in him after so much silence and trepidation the day before.

"Lick me." Simon replied but with a smile.

"I think I'd like that." Kim purred back.

Nick wasn't sure what the hell to say to that. He took one look at Nick and they both burst out laughing.

It didn't take long for the three conspirators to settle in. Simon stepped out to the coffee room and grabbed a quick java and was right back to breaking down what had gone on the day before and how much Kim had found out poking around in all the company computers.

"So what have you told Kim about our trip yesterday?" Simon asked Nick.

"Absolutely nothing. I was waiting for you to get your fat ass out of bed so we could both see the look on her face together. I still feel like it was a dream or maybe some kind of smoke and mirrors thing."

"I would tend to agree but since we both saw what we saw and we both recalled the exact same experience when we went over it in the plane I don't know how it couldn't at least be partly real."

Nick looked at Simon. "Well go ahead, tell her."

"Tell me what for Pete's sake." Kim actually sounded exasperated.

"I've been sitting here all morning listening to this lump tell me stories of his, oh, so wonderful childhood for so long I think I might just believe in Peter Pan. Spill the beans, I'm freaking out here. What the hell went on with you two yesterday?"

"Alright," Simon said "I am going to tell you what Nick and I both agree we saw with our own two eyes and being of sound minds and bodies we think it's just possible that it is true."

"For Christ sake Simon, out with it before I beat it out of you." Kim was really pissed now.

With a deep breath Simon proceeded to explain to Kim everything that he and Nick had gone through the day before. Right down to the moment they got out of the cab back in DC.

Kim just sat in her chair as her mouth hung more open with each passing minute until she looked like a feeding Whale Shark.

When Simon finally finished his unbelievable and lengthy rendition of their adventure a full forty five minutes had passed. At the conclusion Nick claimed he had to pee and Kim just silently walked out of the office and headed down the corridor leaving Simon alone in his office wondering if either one was coming back.

Nick was the first to re-appear and wondered where Kim was off too. He had seen her in the hall but she hadn't even looked up at him on the way by.

Simon just shrugged. "Not sure, she didn't say a word when she went out the door. Let's just give her a couple of minutes to clear her head and see if she comes back."

"What if she doesn't?" Nick asked.

"Well then, we're fucked aren't we?" Simon didn't even look at Nick because he didn't want to see the fear he knew those words would have conjured up in Nicks face.

Those sentiments were soon put to rest as Kim came hustling in the door almost as if she had heard them talking. The armful of plain white office paper was not something Simon wanted to see. He hated paper work and this looked like it was going to be one of those needle in a haystack kind of moments.

"Ok," Kim breathed, "This might look like a lot of paper work but I wanted to print it off just in case the computer files got magically changed. Yesterday when you two left I started thinking about what I should be looking for. When you said that this alien guy, Wayne? What the hell kind of name is Wayne for an alien, seriously, anyway, what Wayne said got me thinking about something I came across while I was doing a little digging. At first I thought it was just another bullshit misappropriation of Government money but now that this Wayne guy told you to follow the money I might just have something."

"Well spill the beans." Simon said.

"That's just it, can't quite remember where the hell I saw it. I don't want to bring the files up again on the computer in case they have some secure protocol on the system that can tell how many times their accessed."

"So you're telling us we have to go through all that paper virtually looking for a needle in a haystack?" Nick didn't sound like he was game for the hunt.

"Save you pouting Nick. I can narrow it down to a few hundred pages. Think you can manage that?"

Nick didn't look to happy about being chastised but nodded in the affirmative and Kim got to work finding the start point.

"While you're doing that," Simon spoke up, "can you give us a hint as to what it is that were looking for.

"Ok, so when you told me to poke around and see if there was anything in the system that didn't add up I ran a search on military spending specifically related to threats non Earth based. What was really interesting on the first pass was the fact that our project has no designation and there is no history of any of our developmental discoveries. Nothing of the well development or the nanite technology or any of the viral advances are recorded in any document I can find. The only place I can access them is in this systems internal files.

So I started with a broad sweep of military project spending outside of normal expenses, i.e., weapons development, which you would have thought our project would have shown up in, ongoing conflicts over seas, anything that the military would normally be invested in. The search came up with an odd list of military schools across the country that were receiving funding from something called the American Defense Research Agency. What was odd about it was that they all received the exact amount of funding.

That got my interests up so I checked the five military colleges in the States and of the five there was one who's curriculum didn't fit with the other four.

Guess where that college is situated?

I can tell from the blank stares that you know its Roswell." While Kim had been talking she had systematically gone through the stack of papers and pulled approximately two hundred sheets out of the huge pile.

"I think what we're looking for is in here somewhere so let's divide this up into thirds and take a look. It's called the Roswell Military College. What I recall is that it gets the same funding but there was no mention of the programs it's directed at."

Twenty minutes of searching and Nick had what they were looking for.

"Yea, here it is. It's a breakdown of the grants given by the American Defense Research Agency and the other colleges have a breakdown of funding allocations but Roswell's funding seems to be going into the wind."

"Let's have a look at that." Simon said.

The Roswell Military College (R.M.C.) is a state-supported educational institution located in Roswell, New Mexico, United States. One of five military colleges in the United States, it is the only state-supported military college located in the southern United States. RMC was founded in 1948 by Captain Bob Josephs and Colonel James Bilings.

"Well these guys are getting funding too and it ain't chicken feed either." Nick exclaimed. "The Roswell grant is like 5.5 million."
"That is serious dough. But how does that relate to what we are looking at here." Simon questioned.

Kim had been on the phone while Nick and Simon had been sifting through the papers. She had just hung up as their conversation came to an end.

Nick noticed the look of consternation on Kim's face. "What's up?"

You know I tracked down the admissions phone number for the Roswell Military College and I got a really strange answering machine message."

"What was it? Simon and Nick asked simultaneously.

"It said, this is Professor Simpson, please leave a message. It was the same voice I talked to when I called down to the hangar there before your arrival?

Nick and Simon looked at one another and in disbelief.

"No fucking way." Simon was in disbelief. "That son of a bitch was playing us the whole time. He knew exactly what we were going to run into when he gave us that golf cart. I wouldn't be surprised if he let that Wayne thing know we were on our way."

"So how does all this run together? Kim asked. "How does Roswell International and what you claim to have seen under the airport field, this Simpson guy and huge funding to the Roswell Military College all fall into place?"

"I guess we start with checking out the college. We already met the other two pieces of the puzzle, I guess we dig into the funding and see where that goes. That Wayne guy said follow the money, so let's do that."

Kim headed back to her own office to start the research. Nick and Simon decided that they had better go and do some company business so it would look like any normal day around the lab.

FOLLOWING THE TRAIL

Kim was fairly certain that she had covered her tracks while searching through the government files. Her unrestricted access was no guarantee that someone wouldn't noticed her snooping so she had used a few simple programs to hide her searches. Using a SSL protocol and another open source software she had made her own modifications so if nothing else who ever might happen to discover her little poking around would have a very hard time finding out who it was that did the poking or what they had been looking for in the first place.

She had also made her searches generic enough so anyone finding the search would not be able to distinguish it from research relevant to the current project.

Now she would have to be a little more careful. Her queries into the Roswell Military College would be such that they would be confined to public record. Still, if the requests were tied back to her computer it would be hard to explain her interest in the school.

Her first search of public documents was equally shocking as it was blatantly obvious. Looking for a list of graduates and alumni for the college turned up zilch, nadda, no one. Her next quest was for specific location and images for the school.

Again none. It was a ghost. Public records showed the registration and address of the facility but no other information on curriculum, scholarships or anything normally associated with a functioning college.

This whole thing was starting to make Kim very nervous. She thought she had an idea of what was going on but she wanted to make sure. There was one person who was kinda in the middle of all this. Simpson. Maybe a quick call to the sleepy maintenance man would clear a few things up.

Kim called the number she had dialed the day before to give the heads up that Simon and Nick might need airport blueprints. After it rang about six times the receiver was picked up. Kim could hear or at least thought she could sense someone on the other line.

"Simpson?" she asked.

"Yes, who is this?" The voice on the other end of the line sounded suspicious. She could hear the hollow sound of the hangar even through the mouthpiece of the phone.

"This is Kim" she replied. "Remember? I phoned yesterday to let you know that I had two guys coming your way and they might need blueprints?"

"Right, Right." Simpson, if it was Simpson, sounded like he didn't really remember.

Kim thought it wise to cover up a little.

"We're thinking of doing a couple of core sample wells out near the drag strip and we may need those blueprints. Any chance we could get a copy to DC this week?"

The hesitation on the other end of the line spoke volumes.

"I think it would be worth my job to be sending those to you little lady. You should tell those two boys who came out here yesterday to be on their toes as well. I gotta go now"

The line clicked off. That was cryptic Kim thought. It sounded like Simpson was unable to talk. She also knew that phone lines could be tapped so she hoped that her suggestion that they would be looking to dig wells would be cover enough. Probably not but at least it was something if an excuse was needed.

Kim returned to Simon's office. Nick had gone back to his own lab to work on refining his latest batch of flu virus. Simon for the most part had been sitting in his chair staring into space. His thoughts, which should have been on the upcoming deadline for completion of Thunder Well and the eminent appearance of the alien host, were scattered and confused. He had more questions that needed answering. He still hadn't gotten past that road block when Kim re-appeared in his doorway.

"Found something very interesting." She said.

"I'm all ears."

"Called the number I got for the company hanger in Roswell. The same guy as yesterday answered the phone. Simpson. It's the same guy on the answering machine for the college number I'd swear to it. Not only that, he sounded, I don't know scared maybe or at least intimidated. I told him we might need blueprints to see if we wanted to sink a couple of wells out near the drag strip and he hinted at you two watching your backs and hung up."

"So what we have is a military funded college in Roswell New Mexico that doesn't seem to exist. A sneaky maintenance man who might have led us down a rabbit hole and Nicks and my word that there is an alien craft buried under the field just outside the Roswell airport with an alien named Wayne telling us the whole thing is a fifty two year old cover-up to pad the pockets of some military elite. I'm losing my fucking mind. How could any of this be true?

While Simon had sat staring he had developed an idea that he thought would be prudent to get into place immediately. He needed to get Nick to rig a second batch of virus that was less deadly than the first. If what Wayne the alien said was true he wasn't going to start some intergalactic conflict over something as gross as someone's greed and avarice. At the same time he needed someone to get back down to Roswell New Mexico and see if they could find this ghost college.

"Who can we trust to source out this mystery college for us?" he asked Kim.

"I think it's my turn to get out of the city for a day." She replied.

Simon felt a little jolt go through his body. He hadn't thought of Kim being involved more than running a few computer traces.

"Common, I can see the look on your face. I'm in this as much as you two. If we get caught my part is as significant as yours. I know as much as you so I have as much to lose. I can do it."

"I'm not sure Kim." Simon was concerned. "If this is as big a conspiracy as it looks it could be dangerous."

"I knew you liked me." Kim replied with just a hint of flirt in her voice. "Tell you what. Find me a way down there that doesn't involve the company jet and I'll use the weekend to do a little research. When I get back we can go for dinner and I'll tell you what I find out and we can discuss that licking thing you talked about earlier."

Simon wasn't sure he had heard right. Was Kim seriously flirting with him or was she trying to throw him off so he would agree to her little undercover investigation.

Trying not to sound flustered Simon skirted the direct answer and told Kim he would talk to Nick and see if they could find a way to get her to Roswell. If they could then maybe it could work.

"Ok, remember you will owe me a dinner for the effort.

"Sure." Simon replied, not really believing that she had any intention of holding him too it. After all he was at least twenty years older than her. What could she possibly see in an aging agency guy who while reasonably fit if he did say so himself was far from magazine worthy. Not only that what did they have in common other than work. Still, he did get a little shiver when he thought about it. That hadn't happened in about twenty years either.

Before leaving Simon gave Nick a call and asked him to stop by his office. When Nick arrived they threw around some ideas as to how they could get Kim back to Roswell with as little scrutiny as possible.

Two hours later they had what seemed like a plausible plan. They couldn't risk another company flight into Roswell so the next best thing was the Cavern City Airport just outside of Carlsbad New Mexico.

Cavern City was still eighty five miles from Roswell so Kim would have to rent a car and take the one hour drive. Simon and Nick would fund the flight and the car rental and Kim would have to do the hard part, investigate this mystery military college.

Nick got on the phone and called United Airlines and booked Kim a ticket for 10:30 am the next day out of Baltimore/Washington International Thurgood Marshall Airport. The airport was located in neighboring Baltimore, Maryland and was busy enough to hide Kim if need be on her way south. Then Simon phoned her and laid out the plan, keeping Kim aware of the danger she might be in.

Kim laughed it off, she was looking forward to a long weekend out of DC and had become truly interested in where the clues were leading. A little danger, not that she thought there would be any could be a nice change after being stuck behind a desk crunching numbers and looking at data sheets for a year. She also liked the concern in Simon's voice. It meant that he really did like her and even though she knew he was older it didn't seem to matter. He was a nice guy and in her books nice guys finished first. She finished that thought and headed off to bed. The morning would come soon enough and a good night's sleep couldn't hurt.

ROSWELL MILITARY COLLEGE

Baltimore/Washington International was busy on a Saturday morning. People scurrying this way and that like a nest of termites that had just been invaded by a hungry echidna. She guessed that analogy arose from the nature show she had been watching just before falling asleep. The show based in Australia showed giant termite mounds and the many enemies of the termite that lived down under.

A quick scan of the departure lines while she waited for her turn to check in and didn't reveal anything or anyone unusual nor did she think it would. She felt confident that this would be a quick trip with little excitement. That was certainly true of the airport and the uneventful flight to Cavern city but Roswell would be quite a different story.

The Cavern City Avis car rental was as sleepy as the city it was named after. The best part of collecting the midsized ford she had decided on was the cute looking kid working the rental counter. At least they had something with air, the short shuttle from the airport to the car rental had left her damp from the humidity and her hair wasn't going to stand the heat to much longer either.

The little car flew along the freeway with ease and the air conditioner was doing the job of keeping the heat out and

Kim's thoughts in. Her mind wandered back in time. She thought of how far she had come from the first time she told her parents she was going to work for NASA or the government in some way. Her mother and father came from what was known as solid stock. They worked hard to keep a roof over their heads and food on the table. They did have the mentality of their generation and so school was never an issue. They would do what had to be done to put their little girl through to the end of college. That being said, they were always quick to flatten any dreams of grandeur. A nice job in a department store would be ok if she didn't get to NASA or where ever she thought she would like to be. Kim had much bigger ideas than a department store job in crap hole Alabama. That was Creola, Mobile County, population 1,926. Hell, they didn't even have a department store. Not really, the only thing close was the friggin Walgreens and even that was run down and smelly. No, there wasn't going to be any sales job for Kim Freeland and as soon as she graduated high school she went searching for a college as far away from Creola as possible.

College seemed a lifetime away from her small town roots and NYU, New York University, was an even greater leap. How she had gotten accepted to NYU was still a mystery. She had applied to every university and college that would put at least a five hundred miles between her and her small town roots.

NYU was a private research university and she couldn't have been more thrilled to accept admittance. It would be so far away and so far removed from what she had been brought up to expect that she didn't even cry when she said goodbye to her mom and dad and jumped the train to Manhattan. Seriously? Holy shit, New York City, she could hardly contain herself when she explained to her parents that it was the place that had the courses she was interested in to become whatever it was she would become. She didn't want to tell them that is was just as far away as she could get. Little did she know that NYU and Kim Freeland would soon become great friends?

Eighty Five miles flew buy, lost in her daydream Kim saw the Roswell welcome sign proclaiming it the dairy capital of the Southwest. Only a few hundred feet further on the crazy alien signs started selling everything from pieces of space craft to food served at the Outer Space Diner. Man, this place is really milking it, she thought.

Kim spotted the Americas Best Value Inn and even though the drive from Cavern City had taken just over an hour she felt a bit fatigued with the early flight and decided to check in, get some rest and start her research on the Military Academy in the morning.

Two star hotels where not Kim's thing but she was trying hard to be inconspicuous just in case. Once inside her room she was re-thinking that idea; old brown curtains, worn thread bare, a shag carpet that had seen so many dirty feet there was no more shag left in it and a bed spread that was so used it was shiny. Obviously that was where most of the shaggin was in this room. She tiptoed over and pulled down the comforter and the sheets to inspect the bed. *At least the sheets looked clean*, she thought, I'll just have to keep socks on to get around the place.

Fortunately the bathroom was relatively clean, mind you aged, so Kim decided not to bolt back to the office and get her money back. It would be hard but she thought a couple of days she could handle. Luckily she had brought a pair of pajamas so she wouldn't be totally exposed to the worst of the Americas Best Value Inn.

Mornings in the desert even in the summer were sometimes cold and even though Kim had worn her pajamas to bed she had pulled the grungy comforter and blanket off so it wouldn't get near any exposed skin. That left her just cool enough to make sleeping a little uncomfortable. She would remind herself to pick up a blanket from one of the local department stores before returning to the hotel today.

First order of business was to make a call to Simon to let him know she had arrived and was settled in. They had agreed that even if it felt a little paranoid she would call from payphones just in case someone was trying to track her they wouldn't get an exact location. If she drove to different parts of Roswell they would know what city she was in but would have to do some looking to actually find her. Simon told her to be careful and hung up. That done the next item on the agenda was breakfast. Freezing all night under a thread bare sheet didn't leave her in a particularly good mood nor had it done anything to help with the pain in her kidneys as she desperately tried to hold on until it was light out to go pee but it had fueled her appetite and at this point she needed food.

The Cowboy Café was as greasy as its name suggested. A typical old school diner, it had seen better days. Her scrambled eggs and ham came with toast and coffee and was pretty much as greasy as the place itself. That being said there was enough on the plate to feed an army if you could keep it down long enough.

Fed, watered and pottied, Kim asked the waitress where she might find the Roswell Military College.

"I know there is a big Military Institute just off Main Street and College Blvd. That might be what you looking for. I'm not sure if it's the college as well." Kim thanked the waitress and headed out to her car. Maybe she had misunderstood, college and institute could be one and the same. She would drive over to the institute and ask a couple of questions.

The New Mexico Military Institute sprawled out over one and a half square miles and was relatively quiet on a Sunday morning. A few cadets were playing a game of touch football on the soccer pitch but most of the surrounding classrooms and what looked like residences were quiet. Kim found the main office and admissions building by checking the site map just inside the main entrance. She had worked up a plan on the way over to act like she was interested in the Institute to register her son. The admission building looked like any other single level school building, widows all down the front with two large entrance doors. Once inside there was a lonely receptionists sitting at a small desk in the center of the main entry. She directed Kim down the hall to a cramped office with counter that held a sign designating it as the admissions office. Another young cadet took her name and asked who she would like to see, then directed her to a little lounge just off the main office and Kim waited there until a very buttoned down and handsome young recruiting officer came and escort her into his office.

As she sat down in the old wooden captain's chair opposite the officer he welcomed her to the school.

"Thank you for your interest in our Institute Mrs. Freeland." He said.

"It's Miss Freeland" Kim countered. "I've been divorced for a few years." Where the hell did that come from she thought.

"My apologies, let me introduce myself. I am Staff Sargent Rodrigues. What can I do for you today Miss Freeland?' Staff Sargent Rodrigues looked the image of military polish and politeness.

"I am researching schools in New Mexico for my son. He has been a bit difficult and has periodically gotten himself into trouble. Mostly small things but the group of boys he hangs out with back home are a bad bunch and I want to try and take him out of that environment before it is too late." Kim felt almost embarrassed at how freely the lies were coming out of her mouth.

"The military has historically been a place to straighten out bad boys Miss Freeland and the Institute has a glowing reputation for doing just that." Kim could literally see the Staff Sergeants chest puff up as he talked about his school.

"So then tell me what would separate this military school from the other military College in Roswell?" She asked.

"Other College? I am not aware of any other military college in Roswell mam."

"I believe it's called the Roswell Military College. I do have some information on it. I believe it was founded here in

1948 by Captain Bob Josephs and Colonel James Bilings. I asked around at the diner I had breakfast at this morning and they knew of your institute and said that they thought maybe it was one and the same place."

"Well mam our college was founded by Colonel Robert S. Goss and Captain Joseph C. Lea in 1891 and we have a four year college preparatory high school and junior college. I haven't heard of the gentlemen you are referring to and I haven't heard of any other military college in Roswell and I think I would know if there was one."

Kim detected no hint of cover-up in the Staff Sergeants comments so she did her own little cover up. "Well I must be mistaken then. It's amazing how you can get so much wrong information these days. Well if you could give me some information on your Institute I would greatly appreciate it. My son has graduated high school and I would like him to attend a college as far from his friends as possible. This looks like a great candidate for him."

"I can have the front office set you up with all the reading material on our college and courses and if you want I can all or arrange for a meeting with your son if you feel he needs some persuading." Staff Sergeant Rodrigues said.

"Thanks you for your time Staff Sergeant." Kim replied. "I will keep that in mind." With that Kim let the Staff Sergeant escort her to the front and shook his hand goodbye. After picking up some brochures on curriculum and information on the facilities of the Institute she sat in her parked car and processed the information she had just learned.

If there was no physical place called the Roswell Military College then the information she had culled from the government files was really all smoke and mirrors. There was no real college and all of the information about the college was an entire front to siphon off millions of taxpayers' dollars and at this point the only recipient of those ill-gotten dollars would appear to be the huge underground project that Simon and Nick had discovered on the outskirts of the Roswell International Airport.

It was now closing in on midafternoon and in Roswell that mean one of two things, siesta or a couple of cold ones out of the reach of the sun. Kim headed back in the direction of the hotel. Main street Roswell held a plethora of seedy to even seedier Honky Tonks and Saloons and she finally settled on a Howard Johnson's not far from her hotel.

The cool air-conditioned restaurant was an oasis after the night in the hotel and the morning's interview at the Institute. After being lead to a booth Kim put her head back and took a deep breath.

"Looks like you could use a cold one honey." A sweet southern drawl made her open her eyes. The waitress looked like every other waitress in every other restaurant in every little shit hole she had ever been in but right now the offer sounded exactly like what Kim needed.

"You hit the nail right on the head." Kim responded. "Whatever you have on tap that's cold and in a big glass."

The waitress's only response was a short "Uh hu" and she was off. Hopefully that meant a quick return with the afor mentioned beverage.

While Kim waited she ran her options over a couple of times. If there wasn't a physical location for this invisible college than the trail was dead. The only consistent link was Simpson. Now there was an actual living, breathing entity she could question. He seemed to be the lynch pin in this whole game. She could only think that if she could track Simpson down maybe she could get some answers out of the guy. Even though Simon and Nick seemed to think he was a few bricks short. Possibly that was all an act to keep prying eyes and questions at bay. A trip to the airport was in order but that would be tomorrows plan, today she was going to get a few beers in and then an early night right after she picked up a new clean blanket.

Kim had picked up a nice warm wool blanket from the Sears store on Main Street before heading back to her hotel. That and the three big draft beers she had with supper kept her warm enough to sleep through the night. It was Monday morning and she only had until three pm to dig up some information before having to head back to Cavern City for her flight back to DC. Cowboy's breakfast was just as greasy as the day before but it went down all the same. She knew the general location of the Government hangar where Nick and Simon had been briefed by Simpson but to get to it you either had to work at the airport or have flown in like Simon and Nick had, right to the front door. The only other option might be to try and gain access through the drag strip bordering the runways. It was a long shot but at least she could check out the mysterious hanger that Nick and Simon had described in their account of their alien adventure. If she couldn't get to the hangar where she thought Simpson might be at least she could poke around there.

Kim knew that if Nick and Simon heard the plan they would have nixed it immediately. What the hell, why should they have all the fun. If nothing else it would put to rest her skepticism about the Wayne slash giant underground alien space craft story. The whole thing sounded just too farfetched. Even if they were working on something that would inevitably involve aliens or something from outer space according to the people who were running Thunderwell, she had always not quite believed in the whole thing. Seriously, how could it possibly be true? The only thing she could see that had any hard proof was the discrepancy in the paper work that involved the Roswell Military College. That was something she could sink her teeth into. These last thoughts pushed to the back of her mind as she headed out East Main Street and then onto Hobson where it connected to Will Rogers Road, then just followed Will Rogers to the Roswell Drag strip. Kim thought it was kinda crazy that she could just drive right up to the drag strip and that that the strip was separated from the runways by only a very short fence. That part of Nick and Simon's story certainly was true. There were a couple of access roads that led to a number of buildings on the site. Simon had said that the one they became trapped in had a trailer home parked right behind it. Kim could see that one of the buildings did have a trailer parked behind in a sense, the road she was on actually separated the trailer from the building. She just drove up between the two and got out.

It was only a little after eleven am but the sun had already started to heat the place up. The drag strip was totally exposed to the elements with only the few buildings huddled along the track to offer any reprieve from the broiling heat. Kim quickly moved from the car to the front of the trailer. Even though it looked rundown it still looked like it had been used recently. The door at least was locked when she tried it. Kim was not going to do any breaking and entering to prove Simon and Nick's story so she hurried across the road to the back of the hangar. It was smaller than what she had imagined from the story the boys had told but the second she put her hand on the door she could feel a strange vibration. The knob turned easily in her hand and the door swung open leading her into the dark interior. Her first hesitant step inside brought the faint buzz she had felt outside to an intensity that threatened to make her throw up. She was about to turn and leave when the lights went out. Her lights that is. Someone or something had cracked her just behind the right ear with a very heavy object and Kim was on the floor out cold.

IT GETS COMPLICATED

Monday Simon was in the office early. It was odd siting in his little glass enclosure looking out onto the main floor. Usually the place would be buzzing along agents and analysts doing what they do. Come to think of it, Simon had just realized that he wasn't sure what everyone did. There were certainly more than enough cubicles each one complete with computer and operator, to get the job done. It just never occurred to him to question what they all did.

He had made coffee and was just taking his second sip when Nick came through the doors at the far end of the building. Simon was reminded how big the guy really was when he saw him walk through a doorway, his head just fitting under the jam.

"What's the word?" Nick enquired as he barged in.

"Nothing yet." Simon replied. "I think it might be a bit too early for her to call."

"I'm gonna get a coffee and then we should go over those changes I've been making over the last couple of days."

Nick hurried off and Simon tried not to think too much about what Kim may or may not have found out.

Ten minutes later Nick was back with his coffee and some sheets of figures that Simon knew would be like Greek to him.

He never could wrap his head around biology. Not just the mathematics of it but he just wasn't really interested in what it was that made snot virulent or how many times a cell had to split and mutate before you got a two headed chicken.

Simon shut the door and took a nervous glance around the outer office, there was no one else in yet.

"I left a note for one of my assistance to bring in some other data once he gets here. He's a great kid his job is packaging the virus for launch so he won't have any idea what all this means even if he looks at the files." Simon waited for Nick to continue. "So really all I did was take the deadly part out of the virus we developed so now it's just gonna give anyone who comes in contact with it a runny nose and the flue. Do you want to look at the figures or should I just give you the Coles notes?"

"You know I won't understand a damn thing about the biology or how the numbers work so why don't you just dummy it down for me? That way I won't have to nod and pretend I know what you talking about."

"Ok" Nick began, "originally we build this virus to be insidious. The nanite delivery system is the smallest mechanical devise in the world. You can't even see the thing without a very high powered, 3D microscope. The nanite themselves have a light electromagnetic exo skin that not only is attracted to metal objects but it can re-align its magnetic nuclei so that it is attracted to tissue once it realizes that it's environment has changed. We got lucky in the developmental stages when we also discovered that under both environments the ecto skin also attracts and holds the viral compound we developed the pathogen in. So not only are the nanites attracted to almost everything man made but they are attracted to man too. That was before you and I discovered that if the aliens are structurally the same as Wayne we would have to test the nanites on some carbon fiber based materials. That is of course if we are still thinking of sending this into orbit. The other virus I worked on this weekend took no time at all. I just removed the DNA strand that contained the virulent part of the virus so now it's just an expensive snot bomb. Either way no one will know the difference unless they have access to a sample and even if they know what to look for under a microscope or they found out that I made a less virulent dose they would still have to put it back together. That would be almost impossible because I didn't write any of my work on the second group of nanites down. They look and act just like the deadly batch."

Simon thought he understood that easily enough. "Ok, now we just have to decide whether Wayne was telling us the truth. We don't have much else to go on unless Kim brings us some hard evidence home from Roswell. I know it's still early but I wish she would call."

The offices and cubicles were beginning to fill up as people started coming in for the day. Simon and Nick went over some other documents pertaining to launch speeds and trajectories something they had done many times before but it never hurt to be perfect. All the trials looked good. They had retrieved projectiles that where launched over long distance, just not into the stratosphere, that showed the package and the delivery system would survive the explosive launch. The rest of the nuclear nations had been briefed and had there now were fifty three hundred thunder wells around the globe. The blueprints for the manufacturing of the projectiles and delivery system had been sent to various steel plants around the world and now they were just waiting to release the virus to the coalition. Simon had lobbied long and hard to find a way to encapsulate the virus so anyone outside of the United States couldn't extract samples and develop it as a weapon they could use against them. Nick had found the trick. Earth's atmosphere is made up of nitrogen (78%), oxygen (21%), argon (1%), and trace amounts of carbon dioxide, neon, helium, methane, krypton, hydrogen, nitrous oxide, xenon, ozone, iodine, carbon monoxide, and ammonia. Lower altitudes also have quantities of water vapor. The quantity of water vapor depends on the altitude. Nick had analyzed the amount of water vapor that each altitude created and developed a way to protect earth from anyone copying and manufacturing the virus by only allowing the virus to live at an altitude where there was no water vapor. That was probably the biggest secret in the place and only Nick and Simon knew it.

There was a knock and both men looked up to see an inconspicuous looking young man with an armload of file folders standing outside Simon's office door.

"That will be Rick," Nick said. "He's a good worker and only asks questions when I tell him too." Nick waved Rick into the office and motioned for him to close the door.

Rick was around thirty five years old, blond, well dressed and looked like he might have come from somewhere in California. His skin had a nice light bronze glow that hinted at days outside chasing waves off the coast of San Diego. Rick stepped in and kicked the door shut behinds him. Nick gave him the lock it, motion with his hand and Rick had to juggle the files from left to right to flip the lock closed.

"Rick, meet Simon. You probably know him as the brains behind this operation but don't let his advanced years and graying hair fool you. He's not as smart as he looks."

That made Simon laugh out loud. "Shut the fuck up Nick." Simon quipped back. They were both laughing now as much at themselves as the look on the newcomers face.

"What have you got for us Rick?" Simon said. He could see that Rick didn't know how to take them. It was obvious that

Rick and Nick's relationship was mostly business and Rick had not had the privilege of getting to know Nick's sense of humor.

"I picked up the files you asked me to dig out of the data base. When I saw what they were I thought you might not want everyone looking at them so I grabbed a few manila folders and scribbled some generic titles on the fronts. Hope that was ok?"

Nick stole a quick glance at Simon. "I was just telling the boss here how you were the kind of guy who didn't poke his nose into things but thanks for the consideration. Just put those down on the desk there."

Rick took a couple of steps to Simon's desk and laid the stack of folders on the edge. Nick had turned to scan the surrounding office atmosphere so when Simon gave a sharp startled cry he jumped out of his seat and went immediately for the gun he had been carrying ever since they had returned from Roswell.

Simon's chair had overturned in shock and haste while trying to distance himself from Rick. Nick didn't see any threat from Rick as the young man stood placidly on the spot, not moving even when he saw Nick dragging the gun from the armpit holster.

"What the fuck is going on?" Nick exclaimed.

Simon was still too flustered to respond but Rick filled the gap. "They have Kim." He said. The silence in the room was palpable but shortly broken by Simon. "He's one of them Nick, I saw the carbon skin on his hand."

Simon had just had one of those moments where time stood still. Like in a movie where just before something bad happens everything slows down.

"I did that to give you a heads up. I didn't think you would react so strongly. It was my way of being subtle but so much for that. I needed to tell you that those that have kept my people hostage for decades and have been bilking your government out of millions of dollars by forwarding false scenarios about alien invasion and abduction have in fact abducted one of your own. They grabbed Kim yesterday at the drag track at Roswell International.

"What the fuck was she doing out there?" Simon sputtered. "This shit is getting out of hand, we never should have let her go off on her own."

Simon's voice had begun to rise not only in pitch but in volume. He caught himself before he actually exploded and drew attention to what was going on in his office. The rest of the staff were beginning to show up for the days mundacity and probably some level of deceit in that Simon, Nick and Rick were obviously not the only ones privy to the conspiracy that was not a recent thing, but decades in the making.

Simon's heart rate and body temperature had risen simultaneously as the gravity of what the situation had become became clearer. Tiny beads of sweat had popped out on his forehead and his palms felt like some New England shell fish.

This was too much. Again the suits had found a way to sabotage his work. He should have known it was too good to be true. Really why would they bring an aging agent out from behind his desk after years of complacency and put him in control of something so outrageous and potentially deadly to the rest of mankind. He had a sudden flash back to the Paddy Wagon. Why had he been so unhappy with that time? Why couldn't he have just sat there till his time ran out and they put him out to field with a gold pen and a pension to keep him warm. The thought was fleeting though because now a colleague was in danger. He wasn't alone either, he knew he could count on Nick, Kim and maybe this hybrid human slash alien was on his side too. Speaking of which.

"So I guess you're one of the experiments Wayne was talking about?" Simon asked Rick. He was taking a closer look at the young man, if he could call him that. He couldn't really tell that the guy wasn't human. He looked so real.

Nick had put the gun away so no one would happen buy and wonder why he was brandishing a gun in the middle of the office. He kinda wondered if Rick could be injured by a bullet any way. After all some carbon fiber was used for bullet proof vests so why wouldn't the application apply? He wasn't about to give it a test in the middle of Simons office anyway.

"How do you know that Kim has been abducted? Nick asked.

"Wayne called me." Rick said.

"You mean like he got a hold of you telepathically?

"No on the phone." That made Simon laugh out loud. "Because we have some of the same carbon DNA we can communicate as some distance.

"So how do you control the skin thing?" he asked.

"Well it's some kind of extension of our sweat gland. With so many years of cross breeding we have developed a couple of pretty cool things. The skin is not unlike your own, it's just that our metabolism is forty three times yours. So we can actually tear skin off down to our carbon level and grow it back in a matter of moments. Wayne can't do it. His structure is still that of their. It is only through cross pollination in a petri dish that has changed some of our physiology. Some of the physical changes we have managed to keep from our captors and some of us have even escaped into the general populous. The fun part is that we can't change our stature, weight, hair color or eye color but we can grow skin. It's surprising what a little bit more skin here or there can do to change you identity. I don't look a thing like I did a few months ago when I got this job and really no one has noticed the change. Oh, maybe a couple of people have thought I gained weight but most anyone who knew me last year wouldn't recognize me. I changed my name too.

"So is she ok?" Nick queried.

"I think so. Your pals are going to use her to make sure you go through with your end of the project so they will probably use her to manipulate you."

Simon's mind was whirling. How the hell did he not see this coming and how could he have let Kim go off on her own on what could only be perceived as a goose chase. The problem was the whole alien thing was now not just a hypothetical idea, it was for real, as well as a proven government cover up. And now Simon, Nick and Kim were caught up in the biggest conspiracy of them all.

HOW TO HIDE AN ELEPHANT

1700 miles away Kim was coming too. As she slowly began to regain consciousness she could feel the low hum that she had experience when she had first walked through the door of the hangar. It was now pushing its way through her chest as she lay on the cool floor of a room shrouded in a heavy blue light that didn't give her much perception of where she was. The low buzz was doing nothing to alleviate the banging in her head and a tentative search of the spot behind her ear revealed a pretty good sized bump. Who the fuck hits a woman behind the ear any way. Kim wondered.

As she made her way to her knees Kim tried to get a better grasp on her surrounding but she was feeling pretty woozy. It took a couple of tries to sit upright so she could see the full depth of her space. It was nothing, just a room, no chair no bed just walls and the heavy blue light. She had no idea of who had attacked her or why and no hope at this point of getting a message to Nick or Simon. Once she didn't show up for work they would probably get worried, she thought but where would they start to look for her. Who could they ask to help when no one was supposed to know what they were up too?

As she struggled to stand up the room started to spin. Kim bent over and put her hands on her knees waiting for the feeling to subside. She couldn't tell if it was the knock on the head or the vibration that permeated everything that was throwing her off but as her system began to stabilize she realized that her space didn't really seem threatening in any way. She wasn't restrained and since she had come to no one had come to check on her or question her. Her first thought after shaking off the effects of unconsciousness was, try the door. Why not? It was either locked or it was not. The knob turned without an effort and as Kim walked through she was confronted with the epicenter of the silent thrumming that permeated her body. It was the gargantuan engine that Simon and Nick had described in their bizarre tale of buried aliens and spaceships they had brought back from their trip to Roswell. It was exactly as they had described it, an immense pulsing and rotating ball hovering over hundreds of v shaped engines. Her skepticism had turned to awe. The sheer size of it, she must be dreaming. It was the knock on the head that was giving her hallucinations.

Kim's upbringing had not included anything outside the box. It sure as hell didn't cover anything as insane as what she was standing in front of now. The most alien thing that had ever crossed the threshold of the Freeland home was a Praying Mantis she had found one day on her way home from school. Her father had promptly taken it out the back door and threw it over the neighbor's fence. There would be no bugs in the Freeland house ever. Still even through university Kim's thoughts on aliens were that they were a necessary evil to make science fiction movies but they couldn't be real. How could there be other thinking human like things that existed outside of the earth's system.

Apparently she had been wrong. If this wasn't a dream then her stubborn stance on aliens was about to be flattened. This, whatever it was sure as hell wasn't from earth and if it was manmade it was the best kept secret in the history of secrets. Kim realized that her palms were sweating and as she took in the giant machine she realized that there where walkways on either side of the engine leading forward from her position to what looked like an airport air traffic control tower at the far end of the structure. She headed in that direction. Possibly there would be someone or something that would tell her where she was and why she was here.

The floor itself wasn't actually moving but Kim kept her right arm outstretched. The whole size and scope of the thing had her a bit off balance and that coupled with the bump on her head made it difficult to negotiate the narrow walkway. As she crept along she made sure not to touch the sides of the space. That would be too much to take if she happened to stumble and touch something sticky or wet.

For all her worldly ways and given the fact that Kim was an accomplished analyst she still had a little small town girl hidden away inside. She hadn't let that side of her personality out in a long time but she was feeling more than a little scared at this point. It was no wonder when a fairly loud but friendly voice said. "Hi Kim, I see you have followed in your fellow explorers footsteps." Kim almost jumped out of her pants. She spun in a circle looking for whoever had addressed her. Where the hell were they, the voice was so close there was no way they could be hiding.

"I know this is weird but just follow the ramp to the end and I will explain as I explained to Simon and Nick when they daringly found their way here. You unfortunately did not get here on your own. You were helped down the rabbit hole and not in a nice way either. After your friends found us out they put more security on to deter any other disturbances. I must say I am enjoying all the company. Come along not much further."

Kim realized that the voice was actually coming from inside her own head. How could that be? Maybe the crack on the noggin had knocked something loose and she was just hearing sounds in an odd way. It really did sound like it came from inside her head though.

More nervous than ever Kim proceeded forward. The voice had mentioned Simon and Nick and it didn't sound like there was any kind of conflict. It took her another five minutes of slowly following the gantry around the giant device to get to what now looked more like a Viking helmet than a control tower. She could see someone coming toward her from what looked like the entry so she just stopped and waited. They didn't move in a threatening way besides she really had nowhere to run nor any way of defending herself if she needed to anyway. Might as well just wait and see.

Wayne, looked exactly as Simon and Nick had described him to be. His outstretched hand only gave her brief pause before she took the strangely carbon looking yet soft appendage in what was surprisingly a very normal hand shake.

"Welcome", Wayne said. His lips didn't really move exactly with the words but close enough and again she had the sensation that he was talking inside her head. "I can see the look of confusion on your face. If I spoke in my language you would not have a clue what I was saying and the pitch of my vocal cords might actually hurt your human ears."

Kim was flabbergasted. Seriously? This was a real live alien. Not like in any movies she had seen but close enough. This one didn't seem like he wanted to eat her brains or take her back to his planet for breeding but he was crazy enough looking to give her goose bumps. She had never been interested in any of the plethora of sci-fi and alien movies that had frequented the theater in Creola. All her friends at the time had tried to get her to come along but she had told them that it was all made up to scare you. Besides everyone knew there was no such thing as aliens. No coursing by her peers could move her to spend her money on an afternoon watching aliens try to take over the earth. Truthfully Kim was kinda scared of aliens. Not the ones that Hollywood invented to trick you into going to the movies every Saturday afternoon, but the ones that might really be out there in the vast starlit sky. She had stoically held onto the idea that there were no such thing right up until about a minute and a half ago when she shook Wayne's hand.

"I know it feels a little weird me talking in your head like that but it's the only way to communicate without some unease."

"Can you understand me?" Kim asked.

"Of course, as you can plainly see we are carrying on a conversation. Be careful though, I might be able to read you mind."

That made Kim jump and Wayne laugh. "Not really." he said. "It was a joke."

What the hell Kim thought, an alien with a sense of humor, it can't be real. Kim was starting to feel pretty tired. The bump on the head and the discovery of the alien engine along with Wayne was a bit much. For all intents and purposes she really had thought Nick and Simon were pulling her leg. It had sounded more like a drunken adventure than alien conspiracy. In fact at the time she had thought that the two men had been drugged and brain washed to hide the misappropriation of the government funds. If she got out of this alive she would have to apologize to the two for doubting them. For now she had been sizing Wayne up. He was different looking all right but not scary. She didn't feel threatened in the least so why not ask a few questions?

"So I'm guessing your Wayne." Kim began. "Can you tell me where we are and why I'm here?"

"Well, you are here I would think, because unlike your two friends you got caught sneaking around. You are very lucky that you only got a knock on the head. I have heard that others weren't so lucky. As to where we are, you are literally aboard my ship and we are buried about two hundred feet underground just on the outside of the Roswell International Airport."

"Jesus Christ". Kim exclaimed.

"I am reasonably sure the individual you just named had nothing to do with this. It is as it always has been a government cover up. All your conspiracy theorist were right but no one could get close enough to get to the truth. Until your two pals made it down her and back out again. After fifty years in this place I would love to see outside again."

"What the hell have you been doing down here for fifty years?" Kim wanted to know.

"Waiting, waiting for rescue."

It seemed like the saddest thing Kim had ever heard. He probably had family back where ever he came from. So sad to think that he had been kept against his will for so long. So sad that whatever family he had probably gave up on him a long time ago. Kim could feel her old self coming back. The injustice of it.

"So how do we get out of here?"

"We don't, Nick and Simon were a different story. They didn't think anyone could find their way in so it was easy to get them back out. You, they knew you were coming here so they were waiting for you, but like I told Simon and Nick, my people are coming. That part of what your government has told you is true. They are not coming to take over your world as they have made you believe. They are coming for me. If your experiment works with the projectiles carrying viruses into space you might be committing mass murder. My people would have very rudimentary protection. Nothing like ray guns or vaporizers like you see in your crazy movies. We are a peaceful and generous people. I hope your friends will help us to return safely to our own world."

Kim was starting to feel the effects of her ordeal and needed to sit down. Wayne sensed her need and led her into the helmet shaped tower where a glass tube filled with warm air literally sucked them up what could have been four or five floors in the matter of a couple of seconds. They stepped out onto the main platform of a huge control room. Kim had never seen technology so advance. No wonder the government was holding this thing in secret. It was obvious to her that they would have wanted to learn everything they could about the alien technology.

Wayne led her to a flat platform at the back of the control room that look metallic hard and not at all comfortable but when she lay down upon it she was surprised to find that it was not only pliable and comfortable but warmed from within. She was asleep in no time.

A BETTER PLAN

Simon, Nick and Rick had been sitting in silence for about fifteen minutes when Nick finally got up to stretch and broke the trance.

"So how do we go from here?" He asked. "We can't just leave her out there under the field at the Roswell airport."

"That's true." Simon replied. "But we can't just go jump a plane and go out there guns blazing. They know we know and besides, you're the only one with a gun?

"I got a gun." Rick piped up.

Rick was turning out to be an unexpected asset. He seemed truly joyful at the prospect of getting to use a gun. Simon thought he would have to let Rick in on their plan in doses. It wouldn't be good if he told Rick they were going to sabotage the flu virus and then find out he was working for the other side.

"You got a gun do ya? Well I hope you don't have to use it, especially if you haven't had a lot of practice with it." Since you have talked with Wayne maybe you can tell us who is behind all of this and who we have to watch here and in the field?"

Rick looked a little disappointed about not being able to use his gun but had no problem in letting Simon and Nick in on who had been keeping one of the world biggest secrets for almost 60 years.

"Well the guy's name here on the ground is Mark Robinson. He's the eyes and ears of the bigger machine up on the hill. Still, he's the guy who puts together the scenarios and budgets to fund these kinds of projects. He's also the guy who controls how much gets skimmed off the top and distributed up and down the line to keep the inner circles pockets full of cash. Trust me, our little home under the Roswell airport has cost the American public billions in obscure funding for everything from making me to trying to reverse tech the engine on our ship. There's also all the funding that goes into protecting the cover ups and the Project Blue Book experiment. Those guys are not going to let that go easily or any time soon."

Simon thought his head was going to explode. Back in the day when he had been scratched from his original project, those in control basically had shoved him aside after his project was cancelled. He had spent countless hours trying to figure out what had happened but at every turn his questions had been met with distain and dismissal, as if he no longer existed and was just so much trash that had to be put up with because he was still a government employee.

This time shit was going to be different. He had Nick and it looked like he had Rick, who if he was truly on their side was going to be a great asset because fucking Mark Robinson and whoever else he worked for had no idea that Rick even existed, at least not in the way they thought he did. Rick was going to be the perfect spy.

"You ever have to go into Robinson's office Rick?" Simon asked.

"Shit yea man, that's what I do. Robinsons supposed job is procurement, I mean, he's the guy who is supposed to handle all the military contracts that get us the stuff we need for every part of this project. That's how he can manipulate the funding by negotiating deals with the suppliers. One price on the paper to be sent to funding and another price to the supplier with just enough kick back to the man to keep his mouth shut. They think that I can't figure it out because the only paper work I see is the original bill of sale but I'm just a little better with computers than they think so I know exactly what's going on. Besides, I report everything to Wayne. We would prefer to get off this planet without being rescued. It would be a great victory for the few of us that are hear and it may save family and friends that will come to get us."

Simon couldn't argue with that. Much as he would love to see his project in action, even if they did kill the virus before it could be deployed, he would much rather have Kim back and see Wayne and whoever else was part of Wayne's world get back to where they belonged as well, preferably without anything or anyone dying or being blown up.

"Okay." Simon whispered. Pull up a couple of chairs. I might have an idea but we're going to have to flesh it out so it's perfect and no writing anything down. We have to memorize whatever it is to the nth so there won't be any way to find us out. Remember Einstein said.

"Three people can keep a secret if two of them are dead." Don't make me have to kill you two.

That make Nick laugh pretty hard but from the look on Rick's face Simon wasn't sure he got the joke.

RUDE AWAKENING

Kim was running. It was one of those crazy dreams where she felt like she was being chased but her pursuer never caught her nor did she seem to get any further away from the sense of danger. It felt like forever she had been racing down a path, darkness on both sides not really sure where she was or where she was going. Just as it looked like she would never be able to go fast enough to get away she woke up. Her skin was damp and her heart rate was really elevated so when she became fully aware of her surroundings it was no wonder she was confused and disoriented. Someone was standing with their back to the platform she lay on, gazing out onto the blue and gold of what looked like an ever turning plasma tube. Every now and then the person looking down onto a complicated panel of iridescent screens and three D animations of what looked like working motor cycle engines. As she sat up on the bench the slight noise her shoes made when they contacted the floor, caught the ear of the person and they turned. As the face came into view Kim's memory came flooding back.

"I'm still here?" She didn't really believe the answer would be no but it was her first thought.

"Unfortunately so am I." Wayne spoke matter of fact and with no hint of sarcasm but Kim felt her fear and helplessness come rushing back in anyway.

"Sorry," she said. "I was hoping that this was part of the bad dream I was having."

"Not to worry young lady. You can imagine my frustration at being here for fifty years and not being able to break loose from something as simple as an electro magnet.

"Why haven't you just gone to the source? There has to be a generator around here that is keeping the magnetic field in place. Surely you can get to it and disable it long enough to get away. If you came this far in this thing shouldn't it have enough power to blow through whatever layers of dirt are above and escape?"

"That is the quintessential the question. Those that are of me, the hybrid children, have no skill in this kind of thing. There are only two of them who are not monitored twenty four seven. As for me, there are a number of exits on this ship but because we are enclosed in earth there is only one way out and that is monitored continuously. Short of a very arduous mining project, I am helpless. You are right however there is a power source that keeps the magnet alive. It would be a simple thing to just turn it off if one could get to it. That has always been the issue. It's just too darn simple.

You should know, I have sent word through one of my children, one that is not monitored, to Simon and Nick and let them know you are alright. They know you are being held captive and probably going to be used as leverage to make them go through with using the blast wells. I know they are inventive fellows so I hope they will come up with some way to redirect the government's plans."

Kim was surprised to hear that Wayne could actually make contact with someone on the outside and said so.

"So if you can get messages and converse with others outside of this craft why haven't you got them to take the story to the press or found someone in office who will believe the story and do something about it?"

"Easier said than done." Wayne replied. "For years we have tried to leak bits and pieces of information while your government reverse engineered many of the technologies aboard this ship. The one thing that has been a sticking point and not in your governments point of view but in mine, is that what would have happened even thirty years ago if I had found a way to get this ship out of this grave and into the air. Can you imagine what would have happened if your world got a real good look at this huge craft? I could not be responsible for the change in course your world would take. You must come to these discoveries on your own."

Kim thought that was pretty far thinking for someone who had been cooped up under ground for almost sixty years. If it had been her she would have pretty much said fuck it. I'm out of here and figured a way to break the seal and get this tank back in the air.

"These days it would just be another UFO sighting and would get some press until the next unexplained event came along. Do you think it will still fly after all these years? She asked.

"I don't see why not. The engines, even though they look metallic, have an organic core. Each engine segments combustion core is lined with a living growing membrane liner that feeds off the heat that is generated by the forces combusting inside it. The corona energy grid has never fluttered once since we were taken captive so everything is as it was when we came here. I have maintained every other aspect of the ships inner workings, the integrated data dashboard that you see here tells me that at the slightest notice we are ready to fly."

"Well then, we gotta make that happen." Kim hoped she sounded more convincing than she felt.

THE DISRUPTION

Simon, Nick and Rick had sat for a few minutes discussing Simons plan to disrupt Mark Robinson and whoever else was part of the great big conspiracy to bilk more millions of dollars out of the tax payer's pockets. It was a simple plan based mostly on misinformation that Rick was going to slip Mr. Fucking Robinson on a daily basis to make him think that the rest of the team couldn't wait to strangle some aliens.

They agreed to meet offsite the following day to glue the whole thing together. Simon for one was looking forward to sticking it to the upper management so to speak. After years of getting the run around it was his turn to send the dogs on a false trail.

After Rick left the office Simon and Nick had a short conversation about the fact that the kid or whatever he was had been sitting there right under their noses for more than a year. If that kid was an ET he was doing a hell of a job hiding it.

"I guess Wayne knows a little more than we think. I wonder what his game is anyway. He has to have something up his sleeve. I mean you can't be held against your will for so long without trying to figure a way out?"

Simon nodded. It was true. Maybe not as extreme as being literally buried alive for almost sixty years but he had spent some time feeling like he was trapped with no way out. His old job back in Detroit had driven him to too many afternoons and nights at the Paddy Wagon. His sense of pride and self-worth had been minimalized for so long that he had begun to believe that there was really nothing left for him to do in life. He had never really thought about suicide but there were many lonely nights and many more shitty mornings where he had woken up with a bottle of Jack still tightly gripped in his hand and a stampede of Brahma Bulls slamming around between his ears.

There was no way in hell he was going back to that. He was going to stand up to the sneaky bastards and maybe, just maybe while he was at it he could fulfill his dream of making the Thunder Wells work.

The next day was Wednesday. The three co-workers met at a pub not from the front door of the Mayflower. The Post Pub was located near the Washington Post building and had been a historic watering hole since 1960. The original building was built in the 1860's and what was now the pub had started life as a tailor shop. For most of the great depression the building sat empty but was turned into a cafeteria in 1934. The footprint had many transformations over the years until its final configuration that remains today.

The Post reminded Simon of the old Paddy. The old wooden bar brought back many a fond memory. If he closed his eyes the smell of stale beer from the taps lined up along the back rail could almost convince him he was home. Well except for the fact that the place wasn't a shit hole. It had been well maintained and was the perfect place for three co-workers to sit and have an afternoon pint.

The room was crowded for four in the afternoon, it would be easy to overlook the three huddled in one of the bright red leather bound booths. All three were lent back, casual, just a couple of buddies having a drink after work. The conversation was anything but casual.

"You realize Rick that a lot of this comes down to you?" Simon said. "You're the one that will have to convince Robinson that we are more than eager to shoot some aliens. He's going to have to believe that because I didn't get to complete this program back in the fifties, nothing's going to stand in my way this time."

"I know what I have to do. After all, I've been lying to the guy for a year. I don't even think he's ever vetted my resume. I'm pretty sure he's not going to figure out I'm handing him a sack of beans when I tell him you two are going to do whatever it takes to kill some aliens. The thing is, you know that Kim is virtually captive but no one has officially told you. They must know that you two found out about the ship under the airport so I say we do nothing until they use her captivity to force you to do what they want. That's when I start giving

Robinson the daily update. If we jump the gun here they will know we're on to them."

Simon hadn't even thought of that. In his angst over Kim getting kidnapped and his inner rage at the shit heels in power trying to fuck him over one more time, he had almost given the whole thing away by being too proactive.

This wasn't his gig. He was really just a down home boy who wanted nothing other than to work in his chosen field and retire with a pension. The pension thing was looking like a no go at this point but he didn't give a shit. He had to get Kim back and get back at those other assholes at the same time.

"Ok, you have a great point. I think the other thing is, these guys think we're just a bunch of nerds, we probably wouldn't consider trying to screw with the big military machine. They'll be so busy taking us for granted that we'll be taking them out of the game."

Through this whole back and forth between Simon and Rick, Nick had been silent.

"What's going on in that brain Nick?" Simon asked. "You haven't said two words since we sat down."

Nick took a moment to respond. "Well everything both of you have said sounds good, one thing I would like to bring up though. Remember I am not only a scientist but I have been through CIA combat training and have done my time as a field operative. These guys aren't doing this for shits and giggles. This has been an ongoing cover-up for decades let alone the fact that they have been making huge incomes from keeping all this shit silent. They are going to have contingency plans and backups for everything they do. And they also know that if they are found out, there is only one way for them to go. That means they are not only going to fight tooth and nail to keep this thing covered up but they would go far beyond the teeth and the nails. The will just kill you to shut you up and they might even have that in mind for after we complete the mission. These are bad men and there is nothing they will not do to maintain status quo."

Simon thought about that for a minute. Nick was right. They had to go about this the right way. Not only would they be in danger but they also had to think about Kim as well.

"So we need to find a way to push them a bit." Simon said. Have to make them take the first step. Once we know exactly what they have in mind then we can start to move forward with our plan."

"I agree. Rick pitched in. "But what would that push be?"

"How about this, you go to Robinson and tell him I don't think we're going to need as many shells as we first requisitioned. When he asks why, Tell him were not sure that we will have enough of the virus to fill the containers. No sense in wasting metal if we don't need too. Let's make the number big enough that it will eat a hole in his budget. That might get them started. They will think that we are holding out to set up getting Kim back. Maybe they'll come out of their little hidey hole and play."

That sounded good to Rick and Nick. Simon thought no time like the present and so they agreed that Rick would take the idea to Robinson in the morning.

After the meeting Nick walked part way back to the hotel with Simon. They chatted about this and that and agreed to stay close the next day until they found out how the news was received by Robinson.

After Nick left Simon at the front doors of the Mayflower Simon watched him down the street until he disappeared with the rest of the late afternoon commuters hurrying into the Metro to ride the trains out of the city to their respective homes. Simon's thoughts were very far from these surroundings. He was totally focused on Kim. How was he going to get her back, safe? That was the priority. He would give up his revenge on the powers that be if he could get his team and Kim through this mess without anyone getting hurt. He wasn't sure how far Robinson and the rest of his boys would go but he would assume they would do anything, including murder, to keep their secret buried under the field in Roswell. One thing for sure shit was going to hit the fan.

ROBINSON GETS BAD NEWS

Mark Robinson had grown up military, his dad had been a master sergeant based at the Pentagon. His was fluent in hand to hand combat methods and had always been a mean bugger. Best known for bar brawling and pushing his friends around Marks dad had another skill that had given the family a little better life than the measly four grand a month his rank could afford.

Marks dad had been there the day the alien space craft had crashed in Roswell. He had even been on the truck that took the ripped up weather balloon they were going to use for a cover up story, out to the field where the craft had landed. It was, in fact, his dad's idea to go around and strong arm those civilians that had already been a little too close to the actual event. He made sure no one talked about what they had seen. He wasn't above using threat and intimidation to recapture any of the so called alien artifacts that a couple of them had removed from the crash site.

When it came time to move the huge structure Marks dad had made sure that those within ear shot of the exercise or those that chose to come have a look at what all the racket was about were taught a lesson about poking your nose in where it didn't belong.

When the true cover up began. The one where a certain group of government and military officials decided it would be the perfect venue to make some extra cash, Marks dad was right in the middle of it. He had been given the title of Combat Specialist, which in his case meant, do whatever it takes to get the job done. He had browbeat and bullied his way into the core of the group and would become the driving force for all things needed to keep a giant alien space craft buried under an airport for a lot of years.

As Mark grew up he had followed in his father's footsteps. He joined the army and though not the brightest bulb he had taken a page out of his father's play book and basically browbeat his way into the position of procurement officer for certain special events, namely the ongoing and still profitable cover up of the alien space craft that had landed in Roswell and was now a permanent fixture under the Roswell airport.

When his father retired and was subsequently murdered in a bar brawl at some shitty little pub he liked to frequent in Virginia, Mark stepped into his father's position like he had been there all his life.

Over the years he had come to know the other managers of the project they were working on. Jim Baker, Bill Nelson, Jim Evans, and Barry Richardson. The two Jims where in as deep as Mark when it came to bilking the army and the general public out of thousands of dollars by misdirecting funds and materials to their own gain. More than once they three had planned and executed huge thefts of military equipment right under the noses of brass. It was too easy and this alien thing, shit it was going to be one of the biggest paydays ever.

Thursday morning had started like every other morning in the last year. Sitting around his office slowly waking up with a coffee and donuts, just staring at his computer and looking out at the worker bees buzzing around in their lab coats or carrying big stacks of data printouts from one place to another. What a crock. The whole thing was a sham. The government had known for fifty years what was going on. This whole place was going to be shut down in a couple of weeks and with the money he made sub-contracting the work that should have been done through legitimate government companies, he would be sitting on the beach in Cabo San Lucas drinking cold beers and watching the sun go down in the Sea Cortez and aliens or no aliens the world could go to hell for all he cared.

These thoughts had just congealed when he notice the kid, Rick he thought his name was, heading toward his office. He wasn't sure what it was about that guy but something was off. Just the way he walked, a bit too cocky or maybe he seemed a little too athletic. Mark had made it a point to recognize people's strengths through observation. One of the things he was quite good at was determining someone's state of health or fitness through their body language. Specifically by the way they carried themselves when they walked. You could tell a lot about someone from the way they walked. This kid walked like he could sprint the hundred in under five. Or maybe it was like he was always ready to just take off at the drop of a hat. He'd have to watch this one a little more closely.

'Hey Boss," Rick poked his head into Robinsons office. "Got some updates here from Simon. Looks like he's cutting back on the number of projectile canisters he's going to need. Something about not being able to generate enough of the payload to warrant the original numbers?"

That made Robinson sit up pretty quick. "Let me see that."

Rick handed him the requisition sheet. Both Nick and Simon had come in early to draft up the paper work that would make it look like they would not need as many of the launch canisters as originally requisitioned. The canisters were essentially sixteen inch cannon shells with some modifications to hold the glass viles that would carry the flu virus into space. They had been fitted with an inner ring that rotated counter to the clockwise spin the rifling in the Thunder Well caused. The counter spins kept the payload from shaking itself to death while in transit (The viral packet was after all a living organism). A small charge set to detonate at a certain altitude shattered the glass vile carrying the pathogen while at the same time forcing the shell head open allowing the virus to be carried away by the solar winds.

The process of creating the specific projectiles was an expensive one and Robinson had made sure that the job was given to one of his favorite military contractors. To stop production now would cost hundreds of thousands of dollars and would cost Robinson his retirement plan.

Trying to contain his anger Robinson barked a Rick just as the boy was turning to leave.

"Tell that fuck Simon to get down here ASAP. And don't leave the building until you're sure you have delivered the message personally."

"Got it." Rick replied as he quickly made his way down the hall headed to Simons Office in the main lab area. He was pretty sure that was the push they were hoping for. Just the look on Robinsons face told the story. He would definitely use his ace in the hole to persuade Simon to do his best to complete his contract and keep the procurement of the original order for the cannon shells.

It only took a couple of minutes to reach Simons office where Simon and Nick were waiting to see what reaction they got from Ricks delivery of the order change. Rick didn't stop to chat, the three had agreed that he should remain outside the circle to keep Robinson thinking that he was the inside man for the government team, so he just popped his head in the door, gave Simon the news that Robinson wanted to see him and headed on to his desk in the common area. A quick thumbs up as he passed the window gave Nick and Simon the clue they needed to determine Robinson's demeanor.

Simon tried to settle himself as he made his way down the florescent lit hallway that led to Robinson's office. It reminded him of his many trips to the principal's office in his early public and high school days. He had forever been getting into trouble. His eager mind was bored with the general Math, English and Science curriculums put forth by the school boards of the day. He wanted to make big noises. The armature chemistry set he got for Christmas the year he was in grade five had been just what he needed to explore the fine art of mixing chemicals together and which of those chemicals made the biggest bang. Needless to say his mother who had been a somewhat sheltered woman, nearly lost her mind with the loud bangs that made her weekends a living hell, let alone the acrid smell of burning sulfur and many other gaseous odors from the plethora of things that Simon experimented with until he got to high school. That was when the shit really hit the fan. Literally, his stink bombs and his aptly named poo bombs where what kept him from getting the hazing that first year students usually endured at his small town school. You didn't fuck with Simon in those days unless you wanted your locker to smell like shit for the rest of the year.

Robinson didn't look up when Simon entered. Fuck him anyway Simon thought.

"Take a seat." It wasn't really a bark but it was harsh enough to let Simon know which way this meeting was going.

Robinson put his pen down and glared at Simon. "So what the fuck is up with the new numbers on the projectile canisters? He asked.

"Don't know what you mean." Simon countered.

"Look don't fuck with me. I've been doing this a long time and my daddy did it before me so I've had lots of experience with piss ant science dicks like yourself who think they know everything and because they think their smarter than everybody else they can just go wandering into secret government facilities, poking their noses in where they don't belong. You probably think that you're somehow going to find a way out of this by shorting the number of projectiles. That's not going to do shit. We have your girlfriend. And unless you do exactly as we discussed, unless you build the exact number of projectiles that you originally contracted for, you will not be seeing her any time soon."

Simon did his best shock and surprise routine. He'd never been much of a bull shitter but he hoped Robinson was buying his act.

"What do you mean you have my girlfriend?" Simon asked.

"See, your already trying to bullshit me. You sent one of your staff, Kim, out to Roswell to poke around in affairs that don't concern you or any of your team. We caught her breaking into a secure government facility. She had been detained and if you don't do exactly what we tell you to do with completing and activating the Thunder Wells, she will be detained for a very long time."

Simon pretended to stutter. "But, what, how."

"Shut the fuck up and listen. You and your little lab pals are going to mix up enough of that super snot you got back there to fill the required viles and shells we need to ward off this alien horde. If it works and we make it through this crisis who knows you might get your girl back in one piece. You might even get a medal or something. Not for bravery or anything like that but maybe for being a science dick or something."

Simon couldn't believe how arrogant and stupid Robinson sounded. Where did he think he was, in a Marvel comic book? He was so sure of himself. That could be a problem. Smart guys usually had a plan and could adapt to situations to make the plan work. That made them somewhat predictable. Dumb fucks like Robinson just plowed ahead oblivious of the damage their actions did and even more unaware of the danger they put everyone else around them in. This type of person often stumbled into and messed up even the best laid plot not even aware of what they had got themselves into until they were laying on the floor with a large caliber hole between their eyes and a a few holes in those around them.

He knew that the first part of their plan was in the works. Robinson believed that he had something on them. Something that he could use to leverage the whole project. That was good.

"What is it you want? Simon tried to sound resolved and conciliatory.

"I want to not see your face back in here again until this is over. I want you to finish the job at hand and no more fucking around with timeline and completion dates for any of the next steps until the projectiles are launched and I don't want any of you trying to rescue your little princess because that could cause someone to go missing permanently. Do all that and you just might survive this thing and you might just get your girlfriend back."

Simon just nodded and got up to leave. "One more thing. I got eyes on you so don't go trying to sabotage the project in any way or I'll know and that wouldn't be good for you. Got it?"

He had been threatened enough for one day. It was just about all he could do to keep from jumping over the desk and slamming a fist into Robinson's big fat mouth. He wasn't normally a violent person and had never been much of a fighter but he knew his way around a bar fight. Years of standing with his back to the wall in the Paddy Wagon hadn't kept him completely unscathed. There had been the odd night when trying to stay out of the fray was impossible. In those few opportunities Simon had found an inner meanness that even he would not like admit to. Anything within reach that was not nailed down became a handy weapon and wielded with enough force could bring down even the biggest and drunkest of assholes.

Summoning all his will Simon walked out of the office. "Got it." He replied but really meant. "Got you"

Nick was waiting when Simon returned to his office. He could see that Simon was really fuming. His face had taken on a hue that he had never seen before.

Simon was just about ready to blow. He felt like one of those old bugs bunny cartoons where the bull, moments before he charges, lets a blast of visible steam from his nostrils only Simons would have come out his ears.

"So?" Nick spoke with some trepidation. "What happened?"

"I got read the, don't even think about it riot act from the world's biggest fuck."

"And? Did he fall for it?"

"Yea, the who thing but he made it pretty clear that they are holding Kim and her comfort level is directly related to how well we do with following through with the project."

"Well that's what we wanted right? We want them looking at us so we can make them think that we are going to do whatever they tell us. Make them scrutinize our every move so when we do move they won't see a thing coming. I have already neutralized the virus so they can look at that all they want and they will never know that it's shit. They can even test it and they will still think that it will work."

"How's that?" Simon asked.

"Because I found a way to make the gene that makes the flu virus deadly altitude sensitive. Once it reaches a certain altitude, one far lower than our projected critical zone, that gnome essentially gets altitude sickness and dies in seconds rendering the virus useless. They can shoot a thousand shells into the clouds it ain't going to do a thing."

Simon was still trying to bring his blood pressure down from his recent meeting. It was critical that they create the rest of their plan to sabotage the program and rescue Kim without incident. They would have to find a way to include Rick in the idea without exposing him to discovery.

Arlington cemetery was gigantic and the perfect place to rendezvous and discuss how they would go about saving Kim.

On any given day there was so much going on around the grounds what with the changing of the guard every hour at the tomb of the unknowns to the endless stream of tourists filing by the Kennedy memorial it would be almost impossible for someone to eaves drop on their conversation.

Simon had grown a beard for the event. A feat that had taken all of a day to accomplish. That coupled with a stooped stance and an old biker's jacket and hoody made him unrecognizable to any who might have followed Simon and Nick to the site.

They had chosen to meet at the changing of the guard. Rick would stand directly in front and one step to the left of Simon and Nick so he could hear all they had to say. Simon had put together a rough outline of how they were going to get Kim back while freeing Wayne and his craft at the same time. The trick was accomplishing both these feats without being caught in the act or getting anyone killed.

As the guard changed Simon went over the plan with Nick in a casual conversational voice, almost as if he was tell it for the first time. Rick could hear quite plainly everything Simon said. To the casual passerby the conversation might have seemed quite normal like a comment on the weather or where to go for dinner.

The plan was simple. Find the energy source that kept the alien craft captive below ground and just turn the thing off.

They would have to find a way to make Wayne aware of the timing so he could engine up and try to break free from the fifty years of dirt piled on his head. They would need to get Kim out before the ship took to the air and they needed an inside man. Someone who knew the place and had intimate knowledge of what was under the ground outside the fence line at Roswell International Airport. Someone who might also know where to turn off the power source that was holding earths first captive alien. Simon thought he knew who that person might be and would put his theory to the test as soon as he could get to a phone that he felt wouldn't be bugged.

As they walked down from the tomb of the unknowns past the thousands of white military stones each marking a fallen soldier Simon couldn't help but wonder how many of these brave men and women had been caught up in some government cover up that had led to their death. What money grabbing scheme had been concocted by those only interested in lining their pockets at the expense of the American. He thought he would probably meet a couple of those people before this crazy fiasco played out.

A LITTLE HELP FROM YOUR FRIENDS

Simon still resided at the Mayflower Hotel and had grown quite attached to the place. He know all the front desk attendants, the door men and most of the janitors and office personal as well. He also knew that given what was going on in his workplace secretly stashed away under the floor of the lobby, that the lobby phone was probably monitored. There were a number of the Thunderwell team staying with the Mayflower family so he was pretty sure that the guys who were really running the operation down stairs would be keeping tabs on incoming and outgoing phone calls made from the lobby. He would have to find a phone off site. Somewhere where he could see if he was being watched and far enough away from the Mayflower and his workplace to so the conversation he needed to have would be confidential.

Washington DC was a sprawling parkland littered with huge memorials and gardens. On any given day there would be tens of thousands of visitors eagerly snapping pictures of the Lincoln memorial or picnicking along the edge of the reflecting pool. Surrounding the National Mall were any number of museums dedicated to the ingenuity of man and keepers of the artifacts of the past as well as impending devises of the future all perfect places to have a discrete phone conversation with the one man Simon was sure was the key to getting Kim back and to exposing the corruption that had surrounded American defense spending for as long as there had been an American deface and extra-terrestrial cover-up.

Simon needed a phone away from the hotel so a walk in the park on a bright sunny day wouldn't seem out of place and if in his pursuit of fresh air and relics his wanderings took him into any building where a payphone was available he would take the opportunity to place the call that he knew would set off alarms back at the office if the conversation was ever found out.

The National Museum of American History was the perfect place. Vast, housing everything from Abraham Lincolns top hat to the original Star Spangled Banner. It also contained many payphones sequestered here and there mostly out of the way of the crowded halls filled with gawking school children and adults alike. The huge cathedral ceilings would have echoed like the Grande Canyon if not for the thousands of items displayed in every cubby hole and open space available, even the thick marble slabs that made up the entire floor of the museum pulled the click and clatter of every day shoes into its stony depths to dampen the sound of thousands passing. The building was old so Simon would have little trouble finding a pay phone out of the way of prying eyes with a view of the comings and goings of the museum patrons. This way he would be wary of any familiar face in the crowd.

His casual perusal of the many artifacts laid out for the thousands of visitors that came to the Museum every year led him down many hallways. It wasn't until almost an hour later, after marveling at the first recorded message by Alexander Graham Bell and canon and artifacts of the gunboat Philadelphia sank on Lake Champlain during a battle between the British and Americans commanded by Benedict Arnold in 1776, that he finally found a quiet little alcove containing two payphones huddled at the bottom of a marble stair well. It was perfect, the phones were at the end of a short hallway that led to the stairs. He would have a straight line of sight from the main floor and anyone coming down the stairs would have some thirty or forty risers to complete without being seen before reaching listening distance. Almost impossible unless they were a ghost.

Feeling assured of his hiding place he plugged in a few quarters and made the long distance call. He was pretty sure who would answer the phone. The one person that kept popping up whenever they got close to getting some answers.

The phone on the other end rang twice. Simon heard an audible click as the receiver on the other end was lifted.

"Simpson." The voice sounded as polite and uninterested as the first time they had met him, playing at being just a simple worker bee, knowing only the basics of his job or the service hangars and what lay beyond.

"Hey." Simon said. "It's me, Simon. Remember, my buddy Nick came out to see you a couple months ago and you lent us the golf cart to go have a look at the out buildings on your side of the airport?"

"Yup, I remember you. I remember you didn't say goodbye too."

Simon thought that was good. Still pretending to be the unaware working stiff. Blissfully going about his day no idea there was a giant alien space craft buried under the field just outside of the Roswell Airport.

"Listen, one of our employees, a friend really, come out there a few days ago and hasn't shown back up. We were told by her airline that she didn't make her departure time. We have since learned that she is being held there against her will. We know you know more than you let on. You can't have worked there that long and not figured what they've been hiding out at the drag track. We need your help. We need you to help us get back in there when the time is right to get our friend out."

There was a long silence on the other end of the line. Simon could hear the humming of the overhead neon lights that ran the length of the hangar and the office where they had first met Simon.

"You still there?" Simon asked.

"Yup," came the reply. "I was just trying to figure out if there was somewhere to hide."

"And?" Simon was almost afraid to ask.

"Pretty much run out of ideas here. I guess I knew this day was coming after you two left the last time. I've been keeping this thing a secret for so long I guess I just thought I would finally be able to retire and turn the whole thing over to someone else to worry about. Bit of a pipe dream any way when the time comes give me a heads up and I'll get you what you need."

"Thank you." Simon replied. "You don't know how relieved I am to have someone in our corner. We've been at our wits end figuring out what to do."

"Well, the higher ups have been treating me like I was just some dumb janitor for almost thirty years. That's right, I wasn't the first custodian of the place. I imagine they think I believed the load of crap they've been feeding me all this time about what's out there under the field. I've done a little digging myself and I know exactly what they got buried in that field. Probably have to go beg a job over to the high school when this is all over but I pretty much had it with these assholes anyway so whatever you need let me know and keep this under your hat so we don't all get kilt."

With that the phone went dead and Simon just let out a huge sigh of relief. There really was no plan but now with some inside help from Simon they just might be able to come up with a way to save Kim, release the space craft under the field at Roswell Airport and maybe save a bunch of alien invaders. Simon thought about that for a minute and then burst out laughing. It couldn't be more fucked up and farfetched if he had read it in a comic book or seen it in a movie. Conspiracy up the wazoo, aliens, Simon to the rescue. That was the funniest part of all.

His attention was suddenly drawn away from his meanderings as he noticed a familiar face crossing the gallery twenty feet from where he was ensconced. His position in the last of three phone booths left him partially under the stairwell and out of sight of anyone walking the gallery so he had a pretty clear view of the comings and goings of the museum patrons from his seat and this particular person was someone he knew.

In the beginning Simon spent almost every waking hour in the thralls of his work. Often last out of the office below the hotel he would sometimes have a quick chat with the front door security on his way out. The team of two changed every couple of weeks and there didn't seem to be any kind of rotation, he never saw a team twice. One night he had already had his little tongue wag with the guard and had had made his way onto the elevator that would take him up to the lobby level of the hotel. He stuck his hand in his pocket to get the pass key that was needed to open the opposing door of the agencies elevator and realized he had left it in his desk. Something he never did because there were harsh reprimands for the loss of any key or access code that related to the business being done under the floors of the Hotel.

Just as the door was about to close he crab walked quickly back into the hallway between the elevator and the only access point that he knew of for the office. The guard gave him a suspicious eyeballing but when he explained that he had left his key inside and would he please not mention the event to anyone the guard relented and let him back in. He hurried to his desk and had just pulled the offending key from the top left drawer when he heard a little shuffling noise behinds him. It gave him a bit of a start but not as much as turning to find a pistol pointed at his head.

"What are you doing?" The man holding the gun demanded. He was obviously dressed in a guards uniform but wasn't one of the two at the front door.

"I work here" Simon replied, "and I just came back to retrieve something I left in my office that I needed to get into my hotel room."

"Hold it out." The guard demanded. Simon wasn't going to argue so he held the key out so the guard could see.

"You scared the shit out of me." The guard spoke lowering his gun at the same time. I thought you might have snuck in somehow and hidden away somewhere until everyone had left so you could steal some secrets or something."

Simon would have a good chuckle at that later but for right now he just wanted to get the hell out of there in one piece.

"Well nope, just forgetful. You can walk to the door with me and check my creds with the two at the front. I'm pretty sure they'll vouch for me."

That was just what the guy did. Walked him to the door checked him with the guards on duty there and then turned back into the gloom of the office without a see you later or a fuck you.

That was the last time Simon had seen the guy. It had probably been four months since the incident but here he was. Walking along in the Museum like he just happened to be there the exact same day as Simon happened to be using the place to make a phone call.

T MINUS SOMETHING

No one had been told an exact date for the alien invasion. They had been given approximately a year to re-invent Thunder Well and come up with a way to use it as a weapon against the oncoming hordes.

The year was almost up and no one had said a word about when they thought they would be called to action. The time must be near if they were holding Kim ransom for their co-operation. Simon had informed Nick of the conversation he had had with Simpson.

"That's great that the guy is on board but he seemed a bit vague don't you think?" Nick asked. Simpson hadn't been the most outgoing nor helpful guy the first time that they met. Maybe that was part of his act.

"We can't really pressure him." Simon replied. "He really is the only ally we have at the moment. We just have to hope his actions far exceed his demeanor.

"You know that when launch day comes you and I are not going to go unnoticed if we don't show up to manage the systems. And I think we will have to have some kind of an exit plan not only to get to Roswell but to get the hell out of here when they find out we sabotaged the virus."

"Ya Nick, the more I think about it the more it feels impossible to do."

"We still have Rick." With all the running around trying to manage the project, Kim's abduction, keeping Robinson from learning of their plans and just generally going about the day like nothing was going on Simon had almost forgotten about Rick. Now he realized the Rick was going to be their Ace in the hole. If Rick kept to himself and stayed out of site he could be the one person that knew everything and would not be missed in the big scheme of things.

Simpson and Rick, one a seemingly dim whited janitor trying to get to his pension keeping one of the biggest secrets in American history and the other a half breed alien test tube kid who probably didn't really know where his loyalties lay. A match made in heaven if he'd ever seen one Simon thought, then laughed. What the fuck was he thinking when he took this hair brained job. He was thinking this would be his last kick at the cat. A chance to prove that he was really on to something back in the fifties when he first started the Thunder Well experiment. Sure they fucked him around the first time but what made him think they weren't going to do it again this time. His ego. He just couldn't go happily into that dark night that was a lonely bar stool at the Paddy Wagon. No he had to show them he was right. He had to get them back for all the shitty desk jobs and paper work they had thrown at him over the years. Well he was still going to get them back even if it killed him. This time he wasn't just going to be the yes man. No, he would find a way, this time he was going to work it out and all those ass holes that were still trying to push him around were going to be pretty fuckin surprised.

He knew that a lot of what would happen in the next few days was reliant on Nick, Rick and now the janitor Simpson. How each of them did their part would determine the outcome of the day. Either way now that they had successfully altered the virus no aliens were going to die but he still had a nagging thought that maybe Wayne had hoodwinked them. Maybe the boys from the other side of the Moon were really coming to do some damage not just pick up a long lost comrade.

Only time would tell and there was very little of that when they didn't really know when that time would be.

IT'S ON

That time came the next day. Simon had been sitting in his office mulling over every angel of attach. No matter how he looked at it he could see no possible way to work all the angles. So many twists and turns he had to find the crack in the armor, some little thing that would bring all the pieces together so they could get Kim back, free Wayne and screw over Robinson and his band of merry men.

He had been staring into space since about eight thirty this morning. His coffee had gone cold a thin film had formed over the top making it too disgusting to drink when the phone on his desk rang and startled him out of his revelry.

It was Robinson. "All right smart guy, it's on, here's your chance to prove how smart you really are. You do this right and you'll get your little girl back and you and your pals will be big heroes might even get yourselves a medal. Conference room in ten." The phone went dead.

Simon met Nick in the hall his mind whirling. "This won't give us a lot of time Nick. We're doing to have to do some pretty fast thinking."

"Fast thinking is what I do." Nick replied. Simon could tell he was joking but hoped not really.

When they entered the Conference room the usual suspects

had already taken their seats. Simon took a look around the room and recognized the original group Jim Baker, Robinson, Bill Nelson, Jim Evans and Barry Richardson. They had been animatedly talking in hushed voices but that ended when Nick and Simon entered. "Glad you could make it boys." Robinson said in a condescending way. "I think you know everyone here except for maybe Mathews. He's our head of security and will be helping you two with keeping the lid on this thing so to speak. Simon didn't like the sounds of that and just nodded in Mathew's direction. "Alright gentlemen, let's get started." Simon had only seen Jim Baker a couple of times over the last year but as he spoke Simon realized that Jim was little more than the research end of this project. "Here's the skinny." He began. "Hubble has spotted an object that at first we thought was a good sized asteroid. Turns out it ain't. It looks like our friends have finally made the trip and judging by the rate of speed of the object they should reach earth in about four days. That means we need to be up and ready in two. All our foreign associates and everyone here needs to get on the stick immediately. We will manage the alerts and the timing of ground events. Simon you and Nick will control the prepping of the wells and the launch sequences from the bunker in Nevada. Your part, as I understand it, will be to launch the virus shells a couple of hours out from contact so the solar winds can spread the pathogen. Is that right" Both Simon and

Nick replied "Yes sir."

"Ok then I assume from the last test firing that we are ready to go. So we will come up with launch parameters and you two will make yourselves available twenty four seven so don't go getting lost. We will also need your data on trajectories and atmosphere disbursement so we don't make any mistakes with delivering the payload."

And that was it. That was the sentence that let Simon back into the game. Right then and there he knew that they had opened up a tiny door for Simon and Nick to put a plan in place that might get Kim back in one piece.

Rick was the only other analyst in the building that was close enough to the launch and disbursement data to be able to pull all the figures together. Since he couldn't out right tell them that they were holding his data analyst captive in a buried space ship in Roswell New Mexico, he would suggest that the analyst on site for that information hadn't shown up for work for a couple of days and that he was worried about her. He knew that their only option would be to bring in Rick and that would give them the inside man they needed without them knowing that Rick was helping them free Kim and Wayne.

"I could get you that information if I had access to it but our data analyst for that part of the project has been missing for a couple of days and we're quite worried about her. I could look at those stats but that's not what I do and it would just be a bunch of numbers to me."

Robinson was at the far end of the conference table but even at that distance Simon could see the smirk on his face.

"All right then, let's get someone to put that paperwork together and Mathews, get someone on the missing tech we can't afford to have a security leak at this stage of the game." Baker seemed almost detached like he had no idea of what was going on in Roswell. Maybe they weren't all in on Robinsons little enterprise. It would be a pretty neat trick if he could keep that secret from this group. As Einstein said, three men can keep a secret if two of them are dead and these guys didn't look like slouches to Simon. You never know though, they could all be preoccupied with their own little piece of the pie but he doubted it.

Robinson called the meeting and Simon and Nick were first ones out the door. They didn't even glance in Robinson's direction.

"Hey." Nick said, slightly under his breath. "That was pretty quick thinking back there. You knew that Rick was probably the only one in this whole place that could possibly get that info together."

"Let's just hope that Robinson doesn't catch on to the idea as well. One thing I was thinking about in there was…"

"How many of them are in on it?" Nick jumped in before Simon could finish his sentence. "I was thinking the same thing. It didn't sound like Baker had a clue. At least his tone of voice didn't give it away. The other three just sat there so who the hell knows what their up to. I guess we just assume they're all in on it until proven not? I'll tell you one thing, I would have liked to have wiped that shitty smirk off Robinsons face for him."

"Yea, I saw that too. Let him smirk. I have a feeling that are pal Robinson is not long for the light of day."

Simon didn't mean like dead her meant more like sitting in a prison cell for the rest of his life. A smirk wouldn't get you too far in the jam.

"Take a hike Nick and make sure your ducks are in a row with the virus. I'll let you know if we get Rick sent to us on a silver platter."

"Ok boss." Nick replied. "Hope it doesn't take too long."

Simon went back to his office and pretty much shuffled paper around making it look like he was actually getting ready for the eminent launch signal. Rick knocked on his door an hour later.

"Hey he said." Looking around to see if anyone was within ear shot. Simon pointed to the receiver on the phone giving him the zip it signal with his lips indicating that the place might be bugged. "Um, the brass gave me the heads up that launch is in the next four to five days and they need me to put the programs together to co-ordinate launch sequences and timing for the whole structure. What's up?"

Simon played along. "Yea, Kim hasn't been in to work the last few days and we can't get a hold of her. They have sent out the search parties to see what's up but in the meantime you're it. We're going to need all of Kim's data compiled and put into some sense of order as to launch times and atmospheric disbursement and saturation timing. We will probably need you to sit here in the tech room and monitor height and dispersal levels and send us feed back to the launch bunker in Nevada. Keep us informed on any deviation from previous launch trajectories and times."

He was trying to establish a reason for Rick to not be at the Nevada bunker facility so he could get to

Roswell. Hopefully by then they had worked out some kind of plan to rescue Kim and release Wayne and his craft from the underground prison they were currently in.

LONELY DAYS AND LONELY NIGHTS

Kim and Wayne had been getting on famously. She had finally gotten used to the sound of his voice inside her head and she didn't even noticed that his lips sometimes didn't move when he talked to her. He would have made an incredible ventriloquist, she thought. Wayne sometimes forgot to move his lips when he talked to her, just because until she arrived he rarely talked to anyone so he was pretty rusty at making it look like he was actually talking by moving his lips when he sent his thoughts to her brain.

They had toured the huge space craft each day Wayne introduced her to different sections explaining that most of the bulk was separated rooms to carry plant and animal samples back to his home world. Their mission was really a fact finding one. Over the years Wayne realized that most anything living, if they had of made it back from earth, would have been crushed by the density of his homes atmosphere. Even a human would have suffered an agonizing, bone shattering death if they had not been kept in a pressurized gravity suit. Their skeleton not being able to withstand the force would have shattered like glass on concrete.

Kim especially liked the giant engine systems that though unable to break the simple hold of the electro magnates, still churned and billowed with energy the rows of twin V's vibrating away expectantly awaiting the signal to go. Kim feverishly hoped they would get their chance. She also hoped she would get a chance to escape as well. She had not seen hide nor hair of any other living being except for Wayne since her capture. She had peered into every nook and cranny as Wayne took her on their daily exploration of the vessel but Wayne had warned her that he had had fifty years of searching for a way out but had never found one. Not one that would allow him to take the ship with him. After all this time he wasn't going anywhere without it.

Kim's other favourite place was the spacious control room. It looked like it could hold a dozen people without it being crowded. She had asked Wayne how many others had come with him.

"There was just the three of us." He didn't elaborate and Kim decided it would open old wounds to pursue the conversation any further even though she was dying to find out what happened to the other two. She seemed to recall something about alien bodies being found at the Roswell crash site. There had been many theories over the years that never really amounted to much but she would have to wait for Wayne to decide if he wanted to tell her more.

They talked about many things. Kim did most of the talking. Wayne was interested in all things above ground. She was aghast that he had not been in the sunlight in for over fifty years. His entire existence on earth he had been buried alive. She couldn't even begin to fathom that. How had he kept from killing himself or going insane? Another question probably better left unasked.

She had told him about things she knew. She spent half a day regaling him with verbal visuals of her trip to the Grande Canyon. Trying to explain the immensity of it. The sheer drops and the orange and umber hues of the rock and how the sun cast arcing shadows down into the canyon as it slowly sank below the horizon. Another day she spent trying to bring to life the Rocky Mountains of Canada as she remembered it from a spring break trip. How the pine trees smelled in the mornings the sheer ruggedness of the opposing cliffs and the ornate dining rooms and hallways of the CP Rail hotels that linked the Trans Canadian Railway from the prairie's on one side to the Atlantic Ocean on the other. She explained the extremes of the cold mountain lakes fed by melting glacial run off to the geothermal heat of the hot pools where tourists came by the thousand to relax and ease road weary bones before continuing their mountain adventures.

If Wayne grew tired of her tales he didn't show it. Sitting quietly listening taking in every small detail of places he would likely never see. He would ask questions about the people who lived in these places or the types of dwellings they lived in. What kinds of animals lived there but to Kim it felt like he was just happy to hear the sound of another voice. Even if he wasn't used to seeing the lips move at the same time sound came out.

She asked Wayne about his home. What the people were like and how they lived. Did they have cities, did they have jobs and holidays? What was their society like in general? All the things she could think of that made earth what it was she asked him of his world.

Wayne never tired of talking about his home. He rambled at length about the way he lived there. In many ways his people's wants hopes and values were much like those of earths. They too had mountain ranges but not as tall or as rugged he thought. Many things on his world were defined by the immense gravity. Some things could only get so high.

Only once did Wayne hesitate in answering her questions. The day she asked if he had left any family behind. He had started to say yes and it looked like he would continue to speak but his words stopped in midair. It was, after all the years, something he could not talk about.

Kim sensed his reticence to bring up his family so she jumped right in with a full blown description of hers and the life she had led in Creola, Mobile County. Wayne looked relieved but his interest in her ramblings never regained the intensity it had earlier in the day.

One thing they had not talked about was how the hell they were going to get out of the situation they were both in. Kim was new to the underground detention center but she was damned it she would be kept prisoner for much longer. Wayne had commitments to his ship. Unless he could find a way to free it he would stick with it until he was free or dead and according to him people lived a hell of a lot longer on his planet than most did on earth and given the reprieve of a lesser gravity who knew how long he might go.

Kim was going to have to try and convince him to help her get out. If he didn't want to leave his ship behind there was nothing she could do about that but there was no way she wasn't going to give it a shot.

Wayne was the brains. She needed to get him on board. If he was going to go down with his ship that was all well and good but he needed to help her plan a getaway. They surely would have noticed that she was not back at work and she could only speculate how Simon & Nick were explaining her absence. It would be a lot easier if they ever saw their captors. The galley of the ship was always magically stocked. Wayne had told her that it had taken him about twenty years after his own food stores ran out to get onto eating earth food. He wondered out loud about whether his carbon fiber bone structure could take too many more years of the salt, sugar and carbohydrates that made up just about every food stuff he had access too for the last thirty years.

Kim had tried unsuccessfully to get Wayne talking about a way out. She had thrown a couple of scenarios his way but he didn't bite. It was looking like she was on her own to come up with an escape plan. She had also wondered if Simon and Nick realized how much trouble not only she but they were in.

PLANET NUMBER EIGHT

It wasn't the best title for a plan of action but both Nick and Simon felt it was probably stupid enough to fool Robinson. They weren't sure how many of the big circle were in Robinson's group but it was likely a good enough name that if seen the plan would look like part of the Thunder Well program.

As Simon had suspected Robinson had assigned Rick to rally the paperwork for the project and he had asked Rick while he was at it to keep him in the loop so he knew everything that was going on including, since he (Rick) was working side by side with Simon and Nick, what they were up to at all times as well. He had no idea that Rick was not on his team.

Nick and Simon had solved two parts of the puzzle. The virus was fixed and they had their inside man. Now, how the hell would they get Kim out of harm's way?

Planet Number Eight was the code title for their plan to sabotage the program. Not enough so they wouldn't be able to fly the shells but enough so no one got hurt and someone would get caught with their hand in the cookie jar. Rick gave it the name after he found a reference to a planet number eight in the data that Kim had been amassing over the course of the year.

Neptune was the eighth planet from the sun so they could reference the plan and there would still be some legitimate data that could be referred back to if found out.

Simpson was pivotal to the plan. They were putting a lot of hope into him being on their side. Simon had reservations about Simpson's ability to put two and two together and come up four but he was really all they had. Sure, Rick was really one of them so he should have been the real insider but as he explained to them, he was brought up in a traditional American home. He hadn't found out that he was part of a crazy government hybrid breeding system until he was half way through grade eleven.

He had needed a photograph for a school project. Something that was on old time photo created by light or electromagnetism. He had no idea until he picked up a shoe box full of black and white photos that he was any different than his fellow housemates. As he started filing through the images he watched for torn and rounded edging. This was the worn out look he needed for his project. He started to feel light headed about the fourth image in. His hands were shaking and he thought he would pass out. He put the box down and immediately the shaking stopped. He hoped that there wasn't some kinda killer mold on the old documents and pics. He left the pictures where he had tossed them and explored the bottom of the box.

The last thing in it was a thin but sturdy metal sheath that protected a group of ten documents. What was written on those pages freaked him out. It was like some kind of twilight zone episode.

The contents broke down in great detail how Rick had been created, from what DNA strands to how they should deal with any odd behavioral problems should they arise. Under no circumstances were they allowed to tell anyone including Rick who he really was or how he had come to be. For all intents and purposes he was an adopted human child.

He scrambled through the old photo's again looking for anything that represented a baby picture. There was nothing before one year old. As he went through the contents of the shoe box for the third time he got the odd feeling again. Like he was going to fall over. He put it down to shock. It wasn't until years later that he found out that it was the electromagnetism part of the photos that was causing his distress. He would ultimately find out from Wayne, once he was old enough to develop a sense of his other siblings and his father, that any electromagnetic force small or large had an immediate effect not only on their carbon fiber skeletons but on their propulsion systems as well. Small force like that on the old photos could give someone with Ricks make up a feeling of unease to dizziness where something like

Wayne's craft needed a much larger charge.

To keep an object the size of the space ship under the Roswell airfield would take some pretty damn big generators. Those would be hard to conceal even in a field full of hangars and old warehouses.

It wasn't too long after that Rick began to explore who he was all the time keeping the fact that he had found the documents in the photo box a secret. It took a couple of years but he began to be able to manipulate his skin structure. Thanks to his genetic makeup his metabolism was insane. He could literally cut his skin, move it around and have it heal in minutes. Over the years he perfected the process so he didn't have to cut himself he could change the shape of his outer skin by manipulating the carbon skeleton under the flesh to give it more bulk or thin it out. This manipulation made it possible for him to change the shape of his face in minutes. Slicked back hair and a pair of glasses and even his classmates couldn't tell who he was. A neat little trick that he had used a number of times when researching his heritage.

Rick brought the paperwork that Kim had stored on her computer to Simons office. Nick stopped in and the three pretended to pour over the documents while writing notes on scraps of paper to keep their plan from being heard. They were certain now that the office was bugged. They commented on different aspects of the launch. Idle prater as all three knew the project inside and out. The notes posed various scenarios to get Kim back from Roswell.

They hadn't heard anything from Simpson since Simon had phoned him from the museum. If he didn't respond soon they would have to find a way around the security and the system that generated the electromagnet field, both were practically invisible except for the vibrating floor they had discovered at the drag stip.

It was coming down to the crunch only a couple of days left. They would need a plan by tomorrow or it was going to be very difficult to make a move in the heat of the launch. It would be even more difficult to move once it was discovered that the flu bombs weren't going to work. Simon slid a note onto the pile of papers on his desk for Rick and Nick.

Let's try to come up with something overnight and define a course of action in the morning. The note read. The two heads nodded and the meeting broke up. Nick off to the lab, Rick off to give Robinson an update and Simon to the bar upstairs in the hotel.

The bar in the Mayflower wasn't the Paddy but it was becoming almost as familiar. Simon even had a favourite seat. He could almost swear that his ass fit that chair like the one he had left behind in the corner of the Paddy Wagon. This evening he was lost in thought. How had this thing gotten so fucked up. It felt like this was his legacy. He could only get so close and then his dreams were whisked away like so much poplar fluff on a summer wind. He had been staring in to the bottles of liqueur and whisky that lined the back of the ninety year old bar waiting for an epiphany, some flash of brilliance that would show him a way to finish what he had started and put that asshole Robinson and anyone else who was part of his shit show on the rails. It was like coming up from a well. The voice in his ear felt hollow and far away.

"I've seen you around here quite a bit. Do you live at the hotel?" Simon snapped out of his revelry as his eyes focused in the direction of the disembodied voice.

"What's that?" he felt like he had been sleeping. One of those shitty hot summer night kind of sleeps where you can only doze until the sweat rolling down your back wakes you up for a piss.

"This is my usual watering hole and I've seen you in here pretty often. You look like you were stuck in a loop there so I thought I would say hi."

The guy was dressed in the kind of kit that screamed military. Every corner ironed to the perfect point. The white standard issue shirt starched just so. Simon actually recognized him from the bar too.

"Ya, work problems. Just taking a load off and trying to

sort the thing out. It's Simon." Simon held out his hand.

"Bradock." The guy said. "But everyone calls me Brad." The hand shake was firm and very military.

"That's a bit different." Simon replied.

"Yea, an old family name. English, means broad oak or something. Mostly got me punched when I was a kid. Simon laughed. Brads childhood problems weren't as dire as the issues Simon would be dealing with in the next couple of days but he could kinda relate and it brought him back to the present.

"So what's got you staring a hole in back of that bottle of bourbon?" Brad asked. Simon was wondering if he should spill a little. Just enough to relieve some of the pent up secrecy cloud that had been hovering over his head for a while now.

"What is it you do Brad?" he asked.

"Well I'm not a physiatrist if that was what you were hoping for" he said with a bit of a chuckle, "I actually work for the defense subcommittee. Pretty boring actually. Mostly crunching numbers and making sure the military doesn't buy to many of those twenty million dollar friggin fighter planes.

Simon nearly shit. Was there a light shining down from above? Like some divine intervention Bradock had landed on a barstool at the very fold in time he needed an angel and while Brad didn't look like any angel he had seen in books and movies he was pretty damn sure there was a little halo around his head.

Devine or not in that moment Simon knew what he was going to do.

"Well Brad, since you asked, I'm going to tell you a story. I know in about two sentence's you're going to be looking at me like I have lost my mind or escaped from a loony bin but I can assure you, neither applies. I think you can help me fix a problem that I have got myself into but I will have to take a leap of faith and hope that your one of those guys who will collect all the facts before you make a decision."

Once Simon had convinced Brad that he was not completely off his rocker the two sat, heads bent conspiratorially until the place closed. Simon left for his room with the promise to his new found ally that he would get him some kind of evidence that would prove his fantastical story.

Sleep was elusive for Simon as he mentally analyzed a litany of hypothetical plans to bring down Robinson and those who supported his greed fed misuse of power and government funds. The sun was coming up when he finally had hit on something that he felt would accomplish the demise of his overseer and his cronies while at the same time retrieve Kim back from the clutches of those who held her captive and expose the insanity of the alien cover up that had been propagated against the American public for so long.

EVEN MORE HELP FROM YOUR FRIENDS

Simon couldn't risk using any of the computers at the lab so after only a couple of hours sleep Simon made an early morning assault on the front desk of the hotel and after some light coercion and a few bucks changing hands he convinced the desk clerk to allow him access to the offices of the hotel where he made quick use of one of the computers on the food and beverage managers desk.

Two hours later Simon had outlined what he knew of the conspiracy, the misappropriation of government funds and money and the general timing of Project Thunder Well. He also related that if things went the way he hoped it might there could be the show of a lifetime if someone took up surveillance of the drag strip outside the runways at Roswell City Airport for the next week.

Simon returned to his room to shower and wake himself up before heading for the basement.

The lab looked and smelled like it did every day. The constant low level buzz of the florescent lights and the starched white shirts bent over computer terminals never changed. The pervading aura of fresh brewed coffee barely covered the electric sense of anticipation as everyone waited for the call to mount Thunder Well.

Simon's office was already populated. Rick and Nick had taken up residence and were bent over a pile of papers on Simon's desk when he entered. A quick fore finger across the lips of Nick let Simon know that he should mind his words. Nick took the hint immediately.

"You guys bring me a coffee?" he asked. Simon knew that they hadn't but it was the first thing he could think of that would belay the surprise in his voice at finding the two hunched over his desk first thing in the morning. "What's up?"

"I figured since we are getting so close to launch I thought we should run the numbers one more time. I caught Rick on the way across from my lab and asked him to bring our last test fire numbers with him so we could take a quick look and make sure there won't be any surprises." The whole time Nick was speaking he was hurriedly writing a note on a loose piece of paper.

"So, no coffee?" Simon quipped. "Ok, well if we're going to go over this boring shit again I have to get a coffee." Simon read the note while he looked for a reason to vacate his office to a place where they could speak without being bugged or overheard.

Got some news from Simpson and Rick has stumbled on some documents that might help the cause.

Simon's pulse dialed up a couple of notches. Simpson, how

had he got in touch with Nick? He hoped he hadn't compromised any possibility of getting Kim back.

"I could use some too." Both the other men said in unison.

All three headed to where the coffee pot and water cooler had sat for as long as they had been a part of Thunder Well just along the wall adjacent to the computer cubicles and set back in a small enclave. The ongoing drone of the florescent bulbs and the general hum of the busy work area made it virtually impossible for anyone listening in to hear a conversation unless they were part of it.

"First of all." Simon said, once they reached the enclave. "How the hell did Simpson get a hold of you?"

"He called me on my office phone. Nick replied. "Trust me. It was as big a shock to me as it is to you and I basically asked him the same thing.

"What did he say?"

"He didn't and he must have been tipped that the phones could be bugged because he made vague reference to returning the blue prints that we had borrowed from hanger 12 at the airport and that if we needed help returning them he could flip the switch to get them back asap."

"That sounds pretty cryptic." Simon said.

"It sounds like Simon has found a way to turn off whatever was making the hum at that hanger and I'll give you a hundred bucks if it isn't the source of the electro magnets that Wayne was talking about.

"There is the possibility that Wayne has fed him some information." Rick broke in.

"How's that? Nick asked.

"You experienced some effect of what Wayne can do when you were there. Remember how you heard his words but inside you head not from his mouth? Well he can project thoughts as well. Not mind control but he can send his thoughts from his brain to yours. Not that good being so far underground but if Simpson had been anywhere close enough for him to pick up on his presents he may have sent him some thoughts on Kim and on how to turn off the electro magnets. He can't make him do anything like true mind control but he can make himself heard fairly clearly. It's actually quite disturbing if you're not sure where it's coming from."

"Holy shit." Simon reacted. "Okay, so we might have a way to turn off the magnets. What is it you have found that might further the cause." Simon looked at Rick.

"It looks like Robinson is not only a war monger and an embezzler but he is a greedy one to boot. Unfortunately for him he's not so good at hiding any of it. I found multiple documents with his signatures on them that start out from point A with X number of items in the manifest and show up with Y at the destination point. Because I have access and a security level that lets me see any document in the system. I was able to scan through Robinsons tax returns for the last five years and noticed that the shipments that showed up light at their destination aligned with substantial cash deposits into several different savings and investment accounts run through an investment firm called Military Assurance Inc. which is just a front for some personnel that find extra cash laying around they want to launder. Guess who one of their biggest clients was?"

"Robinson's old man." Simon mused. "Great work. Any way you can get copies of those documents out of here?

"Not today but over the next couple probably."

"Ok, let's get back to the office and give them something to listen to and I will figure out how this is all going to come together."

IT'S ALL IN YOUR HEAD

Gary Simpson had been born in a one room tenement in San Francisco California. The district of Haight-Ashbury at the time was a low rent, down on your luck kind of place that on the outside seemed the epitome of hopeless with its tumbled apartment buildings and tenement houses that harbored the lost and disenfranchised. It stank of disuse and urine and belayed the hidden undercurrent of community and unwillingness to give up that unknown to those on the outside had pulled many of the district out of their squalid surrounds and lifted them beyond its streets to a better life.

Gary's mom and dad where such people. Gary's dad worked the Warf, pier 35. He walked to work and back every day, his hands raw from the salt water that dried and cracked his hands as he gutted fish. His weekly paycheck left just enough to put some aside for the American dream, his own home.

Gary's mom took in sewing from the neighborhood. Her fine needle work was a sought after commodity in a place where new clothing was a luxury and the right patch could save ones dignity for a few more weeks at least.

His parents, while unable to give Gary toys and sweet treats like some of his school friends they did provide a safe and happy home while he struggled his way through school and community college. That college was in Roswell New Mexico.

Gary had trouble with school. Enough that he had been held back a couple of times and some would label him as slow. Gary wasn't slow, he just had his way and no amount of extra classes or summer school changed how he went about it.

Central New Mexico Community College was not the fanciest or the most prestigious but it was what Gary's parents could affords. Afford as long as Gary could get work. It was also one of the only colleges that would take him with the kind of marks he came out of secondary school with. His dad had a cousin in Roswell and he had offered Gary a room while he went to school and found his way.

The second week of class Gary had stayed behind to give one of the professors a hand moving his heavy oak desk from the front center of the room to the left front quadrant. Gary was strong and easily pushed the huge desk across the floor while the professor did little more than guide the front end and tell him when to stop pushing.

The following Monday Gary found himself in the janitorial offices meeting with the head of that department. His good deed had landed him the job as junior custodian and would become a comfortable state of affairs that he would pursue for the rest of his life.

Gary graduated middle of his class. That was a huge improvement over his previous scholastic performances. He had worked the four years of college every night after school and sometimes on the weekends for extra money. He really had a built in career if he so wished.

Three months before his graduation Gary had been taking it easy in the park across from the College. The park was a place he often spent his lunch hour and sometimes the hours in between when he didn't feel like going to class. School bored him. Not in the way that a really smart person found the curriculum slow and un-interesting, more in the way that someone who is ok with their lot in life and just doesn't need to listen to shit that won't ever be useful in their lives so they take the time for themselves instead.

He wasn't really day dreaming, the day was warm and he loved to sit and make up scenarios about the people who came to the park at lunch. The girl with the long black hair and the little brief case was an international spy. The guy with the long beard and designer jeans was a famous song writer looking for new inspiration in the shaded avenues of the midtown green space.

Lost in his fantasies he didn't even notice the person sitting next to him until they spoke.

"Hey Gary," The voice jolted him out of his revelry. "Warm hey?"

Gary had jumped to the left a little before turning in the direction of the person who had materialized on the park bench alongside him. "What the fuck!" Gary almost screamed.

"Hey sorry man. Look I got your name from the school. They said you sometimes come here for a break. Thought I would track you down. Don't looked so shocked I came to offer you a job after your get out of school. If I could just have a moment of your time to explain."

The job offer was a lot more than Gary had ever considered. He had always thought he would live out his days in Roswell. He would find himself a shy little farm girl from the community to do his laundry and make home cooked meals for him and the kids while he spent his days surrounded by nerds at the college. They would occasionally bump into him as he sweeping the floors and cleared the calculations from the black boards pulling the empty ideas from the garbage pales as generations unseeingly passed him by in the hallowed halls of Roswell Community College.

Regaining his composure Gary could only sit and listen to the proposal.

"My name is Jackson." The man said.
"I'm with the Government side of security at the Roswell airport. We're looking for someone with your particular skill set. We have a position at the airport that requires a person of

discretion. Some of our facilities are on the airport property and some are on public land. We want you to come and take over managing the maintenance for both these areas. It's basically what you're doing here just spread over a bigger area. The good thing is these are aircraft and storage hangers that you would be in charge of so nothing would change much other than aircraft hangars have to be kept quite a bit cleaner than these school rooms and halls but other than that, just general maintenance and watching for vandalism.

We are prepared to offer you twice what you're getting at the school and we'll look after your health care and any other benefits you can come up with. After the first year if all works out you'll get a cost of living increase every year and you'll get an extra week of holidays every year up to five weeks. The areas you would be in charge of are Government buildings for the most part so you would have to sign a confidentiality agreement. Not that there is anything secret or undercover but there might be military and high ranking government personal coming and going and we don't want anyone having access to those agendas."

Gary wasn't sure if he was hearing right. How the hell did they track him down and the better question, why?

"Look, I know it's a lot to digest right her on the spot so how about I give you till the end of the month, that's a couple of weeks and you can get in touch with me if you think you'd like to come on board." Jackson held out his hand with a card. Gary didn't say a word he just took it and put it in his shirt pocket. His dumbfounded expression must have made Jackson turn as he was leaving.

"If you're wondering how we got your name you should ask your Mechanical Technology's Prof. He's the one who gave you a glowing review to our CO. See you in a couple of weeks." With that he was off across the park and into a car on the other side of the street.

Gary watched as he drove away, took the card out and stared at it. Smitty Jackson, Public Procurement, Roswell International Airport, 1 Jerry Smith Cir, Roswell, NM 88203, United States.

Sure looked real. Maybe he should have a quick chat with Professor Wood after his next Mech class.

Wood knew exactly what he was talking about when Gary quizzed him the following day after class. Wood said he had been at a neighborhood function and the conversation had turned to how most people came to their jobs with an expectation that they would not have to really work to get paid. He said he had told the group that he knew someone who actually did his job and then some without a single complaint and without the expectation of reward for a job well done.

Most had scoffed but one of his neighbors had said he

could use someone like that where he worked. Woods had given him Gary's name and thought the guy was just being polite. He had no idea that his longtime neighbor was in fact head of one of the most secreted military cover ups in American history.

Most people thought Gary was a little slow but slow was his way of sorting through projects and situations that most people would figure out in a few minutes. Gary took a little longer but that was sometimes good. The day after he talked to Professor Wood he took a cab to the airport and finding a security guard asked for Smitty Jackson. He was directed to offices on the second floor mezzanine where he found Jackson hunched over an old typewriter both index fingers making a mess out of some form. Jackson turned at Gary's knock.

"Hey Gary. Looks like you have a little initiative to go along with the glowing review your Professor gave you."

"Not so much." Gary replied. "Just making sure it wasn't some of the guys in class trying to pull one over on me."

"Well as you can see, no gag. Not to glamorous either but why don't I give you a tour since you're here?"

Gary couldn't see why not, since like the man said, he was already there.

They walked through the concourse and past the ticket and boarding areas. Gary had been given a security pass at the office that hung from his pocket as they slipped through a side door that led to the tarmac and the staging area for the aircraft. A golf cart sat waiting and once they were in Jackson headed out onto the runway and north to a hangar group on the other side of the terminal.

Jackson showed him the hangars he would be in charge of on the airport side and then took him out an access road to the other side of the fence that marked the airport property.

"Now this side of the fence is still Roswell International property but it's leased out. The buildings still come under our purview but this area is accessible to the public. Mostly because the dragstrip uses one of the old original runways and on certain weekends they can get quite a crowd out here. They have their own cleanup crews so your job here would be to make sure that anything left behind would be looked after and anything to do with general maintenance of the property and hangars like leaky roofs or plumbing and electrical would be taken care of. You would also report vandalism. No investigating just reporting."

Gary didn't think that either side of the job looked too difficult. There would certainly be less duties than he had to perform at the school.

"Like I said. Take till the end of the month and let me know."

The ride back to the airport was just more conversation about do's and don'ts around the terminal but Jackson said if he took the job he would get a week's tutorial starting day one.

That had been thirty years ago. Gary had never found that perfect little farm girl and in that time he had learned quite a bit more about what went on in the hangars out on the periphery of the Roswell Airport, more to the point what went on below the hangars. He had witnessed some incredible comings and goings over the years and had always taken the philosophy of hear no evil, speak no evil. It was likely what kept him in the job for so long. No doubt his bosses knew he wasn't dumb enough to think that everything was legit out at the hangars but he had signed a confidentiality agreement that had been pretty explicit and he had grown use to the lifestyle the job afforded him. Smitty Jackson had long since retired but his new boss was pretty much the same guy with a different name and they got on well. Gary didn't need to ask any questions. He had been around long enough to have signing privileges for any supplies he needed and anything that rarely came up outside a regular days needs he just sent in a requisition form and it magically appeared in his office the next day. All in all things had been pretty sweet. That is until last month when some new people started showing up. They had all the right credentials but shit had hit the fan when his bosses found out that he had given someone access to the airport blueprints and that these people had made it out to the drag strip unattended without a security guard.

Gary could only plead ignorance. No one had briefed him on what the protocol was when someone came knocking especially when those someone's had top level clearance.

It wasn't like he didn't know what was under the ground in the field out past the drag strip. He had been there the night when his world or what he thought was his world changed. He had witnessed the internment of what could only be an immense space ship. It was only three months later when the first body showed up in the main hangar. Security had been pretty tight but Gary had clearance and a job to do. He almost shit his pants when he pulled back the screen that had been set up in the middle of the hangar. He wouldn't even have gone in there but it smelled like someone was collecting dog shit and rotten eggs in there so he thought while the men in the white lab coats had gone for the day he would do his job and clean up.

The guard on duty, who Gary had seen a number of times when certain military personnel were coming and going, just nodded as he went to go in. His first breath inside the tarped area just about made him barf up the soup he had had for dinner. What in the hell could smell like that? Whatever it was had been piled up on the table in the middle of the makeshift room. As he approached the stench intensified to the point where he had to pull the corner of his overalls over his mouth and nose. Even with that his eyes had begun to water.

One look at what lay on the table sent him flying. The lower half of the mass was a jumble of what looked like guts only different. Back in San Fran his mom and dad had often had to slaughter their own chickens so he know what entrails looked like. This looked like guts but they were all black and shiny like broken bits of hand polished pottery. It was the head that had sent him running. Its black eyes staring right at him. What was a layer of grey skin peeled back from the forehead down showed not bone and tendon but the same black shiny substance that lay scrambled up at the other end.

Gary exited the room and landed on his knees. The guard was equally bent over but with laughter.

"See something that didn't agree with you Gary?" the guy was killing himself.

Gary could only sit and catch his breath. An alien, a fucking alien, was what he was thinking. Had to be. Would there be so much secrecy around the place and a guard on duty if it was just some experiment gone wrong.

Gary got to his feet.

"You know you can't say shit about this right Gary?" Gary just nodded and walked back to his office not really able to believe what he had just seen.

It took more than a few minutes for Gary to catch his breath. He had more than once gaged on the bile rising in his throat and had just barely kept from puking his guts out. The only thing that had kept him from leaving his dinner on the hangar floor was his determination to not let the guard see him lose it.

Gary didn't revisit the little autopsy room set up in the middle of hangar 3 and in a couple of days the whole mess was gone with no one the wiser. Gary was wiser though and he made it a personal mission, like he did with most things he didn't understand, to find out everything he wasn't supposed to know about the job he had taken on.

Since that day Gary had found out pretty much everything that anybody knew about what was buried out under the ground just the other side of the drag strip. Of course he had heard the conspiracy theories and had even encountered an alien investigator or two in his years at the job but he had never felt the compunction to give anyone any of the information he had gleaned over that time.

He had come to the conclusion that the American government must have some serious reasons for keeping something as big and as incredible as an almost one mile across alien aircraft and its now sole occupant buried under the airport field. He had signed the confidentiality agreement, he worked for the government, he liked his job and who was he to spill the beans.

That was his credo until the young lady went out to the field and hadn't come back. It was one thing to harness an alien force and keep it from wreaking havoc on an unsuspecting human population but it was truly another to imprison someone below ground, an American to boot, with no hope of escape. He already knew that that first and last prisoner in the subterranean lock up had been there for more than fifty years. He couldn't let that happen to anyone else. Good or bad he would have to find a way to extricate her without getting into too much trouble himself.

Gary thought it was particularly funny that the rest of the staff in his little circle of friends thought that he was a slow. They wouldn't say it to his face but they were pretty loose with where they left documents and what they said within his ear shot. They wrongly assumed that because he was the janitor slash grounds keeper that his understanding of everything else was limited. That didn't offend him he had actually finished his mechanical technologies degree and while not at the top of his class he had a pretty good understanding of propulsion systems and anything that needed a metal part to function. It was really only their belief that he would not understand a word they were saying that gave Gary all the information needed to know what was under the ground at the drag strip and why. It also gave him the power of the computer. In class they were not confined to practical mechanics but had started to explore the virtual possibilities of the computer model. Not grinding out parts on the lath but building the entire mechanism in the virtual confines of the computer and then creating the blueprint to manufacture anything they could imagine.

Gary wasn't a geek but he was better than anyone expected when it came to manipulating a keyboard and because his thought processes were so deliberate he often found things that others did not. His slow seven day crawl through secure documents and files that he had found locked in certain folders on the computer in the office were astounding. Probably no one had thought that he would ever use his security clearance to log into the daily goings on in their little part of the world and with a little help from Wayne, Gary had eventually dug deep enough to discover Thunder Well and its objective. He also found all the files on those making the project happen. He also recognized some of those government employees. The two who had shown up a month ago and the woman who he knew to be sequestered below ground at the present time.

It wasn't too hard to find individual phone numbers. He had called the Nick person because he looked like he could handle himself. His file said he was a biological engineer but he looked like the kind of guy who could crack a few bones. That was one of his Moms old sayings. It meant tough and

Nick looked tough.

When he called the number the connection wasn't too good. It had a lot of crackling and static on the line. He watched spy movies and whether it was true or not that was a sure sign of a wiretap. Better safe than sorry he had given Nick a cryptic message alluding to the hangars and to the fact that not two days ago he had found the power source of the giant magnets that kept the alien ship from escaping.

Over the years a litany of scientists, computer wizards and government know it all's had had pillaged the alien vessel. They had reverse engineered everything they could get their hands on. Slowly creating and then leaking alien technology to the masses. Making fortunes in the process from computer chip synthesis to cell phones and blue tooth technologies. Hell the aliens themselves had been instrumental in the development of carbon fiber and Kevlar. Both materials reverse engineered from their own physical structures. The only thing they had never been able to figure out was how the propulsion system worked. They had never seen it in action. Too afraid to lower the magnetic field that kept the craft a prisoner and not able to understand how the energy was generated they had struggled for generations to find the answer.

It was Wayne, the captive alien that had motivated Gary to act. A week ago he had started hearing someone talking to him in his head. At first he thought he was losing it. But the voice had actually introduce itself. He had let Gary know that the woman, her name was Kim, was with him and safe. He also let him know that the time was near when she would not be so safe. That his people were coming for him and while they were not violent and only wished to return him and his craft to their world, Gary's people were not so gentle. He let Gary know that it would be a good idea to find a way to get hold of Nick or Simon who were part of the Thunder Well program and who he had met a couple of weeks earlier and try to find a way to retrieve Kim from her jail. It was Wayne's voice that had guided him through the process of file surfing that led him to Nick's phone number.

He knew it was time. The whole frigging thing was absurd if you think about it. Yea, it might have been a good idea to keep a huge alien aircraft and its crew a secret but in today's world people were smarter than that. They could accept and understand the alien.

It was more likely that the population wouldn't understand the cover up. Some alien conspiracy theorists were going to have a field day. The first time he heard Wayne's voice Wayne had helped him through hacking into the secure system that held the secret files of the Thunder Well program. After seven days of shuffling through files Gary had got pretty far but had run up against a road block. His security password only got him in so deep. There was a whole new level of files that were inaccessible. Hidden away and secured with an encryption code. Turned out Wayne had the code which obviously made it less of a hack and more of a joke and he had wondered how Wayne could have figured it out locked up and buried under the field. He no sooner popped the thought when Wayne answered in his head.

"The same way I'm talking to you right now. I can send my thoughts to you in the form of spoken word but I cannot control your mind. That would be a real trick. I can also hear what you're thinking so when Nick and Simon had paid me a visit there were some things rolling around in Nicks head and one of them was a file he was working on that required an encryption code. Just glad it got us to where we wanted to go."

"So why don't you just send them one of these in your head messages." Simon thought.

"If I could get closer to the surface and closer to them I certainly would but this far underground you are my only hope."

After Gary's little tutorial on how to get into the files Gary had made his call to Nick. Now he needed to find a way to communicate and co-ordinate a plan to get Kim out and Wayne free.

ALIEN INVASION

Wayne and Kim had spent some time together. Wayne had heard many of Kim's private thoughts during their conversations and even though he would have liked to have told her of the others of his crew that were no longer there he still couldn't bring himself to talk about them. The one question that Kim had asked that really was the only question.

"Why had the government kept him prisoner for so many years?"

When their craft had trouble acclimatizing to the difference in the density of earth's atmosphere Wayne and his crew had no choice but to try and land to make adjustment to the engines solar pulse rhythms. That unfortunate incident was what brought them to the desert just north of Roswell New Mexico in 1947. The landing didn't go as planned and the impact not only rendered them unconscious for an hour but the hull had been breached and the lighter atmosphere that had been leaking in while they slept was making them light headed and unable to concentrate as when they awoke. By the time they had recovered enough to understand what had happened they had been rendered helpless by the electro magnets the army had attach to the hull to haul it away.

The army had seen them coming. What Wayne had come to

understand was that the Airforce had been monitoring their flight path from Roswell Army Air Field. They had watched the trajectory and had dispatched forces from the 509th Operations Group in their general landing direction well in advance of the crash.

That group had been followed up by three Sikorsky CH-54 helicopters that the army was secretly testing at the base. This was uncharted waters for the helo's. They had never been more than twenty feet off the ground and were still in developmental but the radar had indicated the size of the falling object and since they were there and available why not a field test.

Each chopper carried a huge magnet capable of lifting the aircrafts maximum payload of twelve tons. The question was, would it be enough for whatever had just ditched out in the desert north of Roswell.

The impact of the landing had done something more to the propulsion system of Wayne's ship. He was still in shock and under the influence of earth's atmosphere when he woke up and was having a hard time focusing on what the problem was. The system looked to be functioning as usual. The plasma array was still up but he couldn't get it to create enough lift to move the craft. Every time he powered up to hover level it stalled. They were stuck just light enough to be off the ground but not enough juice to get airborne.

He had begun to check on the rest of his crew when he heard the first of the big magnets attach itself to the hull. He wasn't really worried. They had been flying the planet for a number of days under the cover of night. They were monitoring the airways and knew a little about the population of the earth, specifically of the United States. He also knew that whatever was going on that they would have a very tough time breaching the hull of the space ship. Its carbon fiber and graphite melded hull was made from a particular material found fifty miles below the surface of his home planet. Even their own technologies had a difficult time creating the process that allowed it to be formed and molded to the aerodynamics of the ship. Ten years of research would make the hull practically indestructible while keeping its occupants safe from space debris and the possibility of even heavier atmospheres than their own. He was fairly confident that that in itself would keep them safe long enough to make the repairs they need to the propulsion system and once that was accomplished there was nothing on this planet that could hold the plasma fed hyper system down. Wayne had not taken into consideration that the method they had use to make a network of covalent bonds between the graphite found on the surface of his planet and the atypical carbon fiber found far below would leave small clusters of heavy magnetic particles deep within the structure of the hull. When all three of the magnets dangling from the overhead Sikorsky's came in contact with the hull they started a loop that set these molecules in motion That circuit would set Wayne's own engines in a locked position that created enough lift for the three choppers to accomplish the extraction of the huge craft and at the same time immobilize it from taking off dragging the helo's behind.

Below in the space ship Wayne and his crew could only stare at one another in disbelief when the deck beneath their feet began to move. Wayne knew that in the state his engine was in there was no way that they were making way under their own power so it had to be from an outside source. But how could they? His ship was too big for anything they had seen or heard of in their nightly wanderings of the planet. He could only sit with his people and discuss what they should do. Should they fight, should they hide even should they kill themselves? He could hear the fear growing in their voices. They had not planned for this kind of scenario. They were only supposed to observer from afar. Now, he thought they were going to get a close up look at this world and maybe not in a way they were going to like.

The combined forces outside the giant craft had no idea that all these things were going on within the walls of the space ship itself and with the crafts occupants. They believed that the three Sikorsky helicopters were doing all the heavy lifting, a belief that would end in losing a couple of the big choppers when they tried to take on overweight carries in subsequent field tests. The next big test was going to be what to do with the craft. There wasn't a hanger anywhere that could accommodate its huge triangular shape. They needed a way to contain it but still be able to access it to glean its secrets.

There were a number of logistical pieces that had to be put together in a hurry.

1. The choppers couldn't move something this heavy too far. They didn't even know if they could take it high enough that it wouldn't be observed from the ground at night.

2. If they moved it within eyesight how could they contain the fallout of people seeing a real live alien space ship?

3. Where could they hide it and still keep it secret?

4. What would the cover story be if found out and what could they do to mitigate that if it happened?

Back at the base a think tank had been set up in one of the fighter pilot classrooms. A group of Army and Air Force thinkers were huddled around a map of the area were the ship had gone down and where they were now preparing to lift it out of the sand.

Where too was the biggest question and how to do it without drawing undue attention to the fact?

Many varied suggestions had been put forward but all the facilities within range of the Sikorskies were too small. The best case scenario would be to hide it somehow. Could they use military camouflage tenting to keep it hidden out in the desert? No. Could they bisect it and move the two halves to two hangars? No.

One of the engineers who had been pulled in from the military attachment to the Roswell Airport suggested that maybe they could sink it in the huge catch basin that was just outside the airport runways. The basin was nestled between Will Rogers Road and the 255. It was part of the mesa that ran east through the farms and roads to the runways of the airport. As part of the original plan for the Airport engineers had dug a huge catch basin to keep run off, storm and waist waters accumulating in and around the airport from pooling in the area of the runways. It was deep and big enough to drop something the size of the alien ship into and they could cover it over with earth after it was in place to keep it from prying eyes.

"What about the water displacement in the basin. Won't that create an overflow onto the runways or onto public road ways?" One of the attending aids asked. Well we need to see the elevation of Will Rogers Road first but I think it would contain the overflow in that direction. 255 would probably flood out as the flow went in that direction but it would clear quickly as the water made for the mesa and got absorbed.

They all looked at one another. Could it work? Sounded

crazy but it was the only idea that had any float so far.

The next big question. If they did try to sink it in the basin how could they move it into position get all the engineering done to keep the magnetic hand cuffs on it and not have anyone see them doing it. The answer was as nuts as everything else they had thought of so far. They would just hold on and see what happened.

IMPOSSIBLE

If you had read the game plan cooked up by those in that little room at Army Air Field that night you would have laughed out loud. I was so insane in its intent that one could hardly think it was possible to pull off. The team of Army and Airforce experts that did pull it off would never be able to puff out their chests and brag about how they had successfully captured and secured then hid an almost mile wide space ship in the swamp out at the Airport.

The 509th Composite Group which had been based at Wendover Army Airfield in Utah had been relocated to Roswell Army Air Field in 1945. Amongst other aircraft in the Group were a number of B-29 bombers perfect for the job at hand. The 509th Composite Group was the only unit that had experience in deploying nuclear weapons. Another weapon the group had access to that was not public knowledge was a chemical nerve agent designed to render mass immobilization of population. The agent was really a mild sedative that someone in intelligence thought could be used to anesthetize a city before an atomic drop. Some claimed it a humane euthanasia and would play better with the UN if there was any fallout from dropping atomic weapons on entire populations. Roswell Army Field had access to this agent and with a very quick refit of a couple of B-29's part of their plan was in place.

Just before midnight on July 8 1947 two B-29 bomber aircraft left Roswell Army Air Field looped north of the town and then headed back over the city and on to the airport. Only those immediately involved in the operation were advised of the eminent forced nap time. Everyone else would wake with a headache in a few hours and would be given the media report that was now being concocted for the curious and nosy.

Those who were still awake or out on late night errands never even looked up. Some might have thought that the aircraft were flying a little lower than usual but with the air field only five kilometers from town it was not unusual to have low flying planes at all hours of the day or night.

A fake tornado warning was issued for the city of Roswell and area essentially shutting down the airport, grounding the planes and forcing travelers to shelter in the underground parking lots. Those few who fell through the cracks and ended up being effected by the nerve agent would be fed the chemical spill story as cover. They hoped the warning would keep travelers off the roads in the area as well.

The three Sikorski helicopters had sat for almost an hour at five thousand feet. Precariously clinging to their cargo, out of sight of prying eyes, covered by the dark of night. Those who might have had opportunity to look skyward could have notices a peculiar shaped blank spot in the star filled night but at five thousand feet in the middle of the desert the likelihood of that taking place was minimal.

At twelve forty five the choppers were directed to move their cargo to the coordinates just off the end runway at the airport and Will Rodgers Road.

Gary had received a phone call at the hangar at ten to midnight. He was doing a little graveyard work picking up a couple extra buck to repair his old pick up that got him back and forth to work. It was the Airforce base. He was informed that a fertilizer tank had erupted on a farm north of town and that he should get his gas mask on ASAP. Gary had asked about the people in the airport and had been told that the army had issued a tornado warning to keep them from panicking and they were all safely being housed in the underground parking garage. His job was to stay on post and wait for an all clear signal. Gary found the whole thing a bit cryptic but at this point in his career he wasn't going to make any waves. Ten minutes later he heard the two B-29's making their run. He couldn't know that they were dropping the gas that he had been warned about. He just hoped that he wouldn't have any ill effects from the gas as he pulled the gasmask down from the storage locker and placed it over his face.

Twenty minutes later the roar of the three huge laboring Sikorsky was enough to wake the dead. From his office where he had been trying to stay calm while the glass eye pieces in his gas mask fogged to the point of blindness, Gary heard the helo's getting closer and then felt the impact of the giant blades as the entire hangar around him began to shake and quiver with the downdraft. The noise was deafening. It really did sound like a hurricane. He had been around long enough to know the difference between a huge wind and a huge machine so even though his vision was impaired in the mask, Gary found his way to the back door of the hangar and looked out over the fence that defined the airport property. As he struggled to see through the condensation that had formed on his eye pieces he saw an enormous black shape beginning to appear out of the night sky just on the other side of Will Rodgers road. What the fuck is this? He thought. This was no hurricane and he was pretty damn sure there was no chemical emergency either. As he watched the object came closer and closer to the ground he could make out the three helicopters that controlled its decent.

The lowering of the space craft while controlled was not as precise as the pilots of the three choppers would have liked. The impact as it splashed down into the containment pond sent displacement waves up over Will Rodgers road on one side and an even bigger wave to the downside and into the mesa beyond. The wave almost toppled the six large dump trucks and a whole division of earth moving equipment lined up along the perimeter road.

The ship was still somewhat buoyant as its troubled

propulsion system struggled to maintain but the effect of the three large magnets was effectively keeping the process from gaining any momentum.

The ship was losing ground and as it started to sink into the basin it became level with the surrounding berm. When the hull became leveled with the road the six big dump trucks drove onto its back. Their combined weight was enough to force the ship slowly down into the lake and the muck and ooze below. So followed the dump trucks as their life vested drivers jumped from the sinking cabs and grabbed waiting throw lines from the shore. Next the parking lot of earth movers went to work. Their only job was to back fill the space as the craft sank further into the lake. Dump trucks full of earth from the local gravel pit began pulling onto Will Rodgers Road to deposit the earth necessary to completely bury the ship. One after another as the craft eventually became covered. An hour and a half later the whole field looked nothing more than a construction site being readied for new hangars or a parking lot. In turn the choppers released their umbilical cords to the magnets that were swiftly re-attached to waiting generators housed in waiting big rig trucks.   The phone was ringing in Gary's office. It took a few rings to wake him out of his revelry. If was Bradock, his boss.

"Quite the show eh Gary?"

"What's going on?" Gary stammered. It felt like he had

been punched in the chest. Did he really see what he thought he saw?

Bradock assured him that he had. He also reminded him that he could not say a word of it to anyone ever. The terms of his contract were explicit and if he did decide to spill the beans Bradock reminded him that treason was still a crime punishable by death in New Mexico.

Gary fell asleep in his office that night and woke up cramped and a little disoriented. He was about to put it all off as a crazy dream until he saw the gas mask hastily discarded the night before, laying on the floor near his desk. Out by the drag strip the new day saw the birth of an almost two thousand square foot field. Unseen from above the ship had filled and then some the six story hole where once the water of the catch basin sat. Now the entire area was covered with ten feet of rock, rubble and back frill.

DIVERSION

Rick had told Simon that Robinson was sure they were planning to sabotage the Thunder Well project. He had as much told him that they would be detained before the launch of any of the projectiles. He did however not know that they had already essentially rendered the virus ineffectual. He also could not know that even if the virus was tested at ground level it would still test viral. It would only be with attained altitude that it would become useless.

The information gave Simon an idea. They should come up with a decoy plan and let Robinson discover it to throw him off their real intent. It had to be plausible something Robinson would fall for hook line and sinker.

Nick was the one who thought of the perfect plot. Since the virus was going to become useless at a certain altitude why not actually take the virulent pathogen component out of their virus. Then leak the fact to Robinson. Let Rick tell him that he thinks the team is going to make the formula inert by removing it. That will make Rick look like an asset to Robinson and Robinson will get one of the other lab techs to put the pathogen back into the formula. He will think he has foiled our plot and as long as he thinks we don't know that he is going to detain us he will believe he has his T's crossed.

It really was a great idea and kinda funny at the same time. Nick immediately reworked the formulas that were waiting to be fed into the launch viles to omit the pathogen. Rick waited most of the day before reporting in with Robinson and revealing his suspicions.

They all headed for home around the same time and as they passed in the common room on their respective trajectories Rick caught Simon's eye and gave him a wink. The fix was in. They would just have to wait and see if Robinson took the bait. Simon hoped he would. The shop was buzzing today. Something was up and he was pretty sure that they weren't too far off launch. They would probably be kept in the dark until that last minute so they couldn't pull any funny business. It didn't matter, the funny stuff was already pulled.

Simon slept like a baby. The last few days had run his nerves ragged. He hadn't heard back from Bradock about the information he had left for him at the bar in the Mayflower but he didn't really expect too.

The next morning Simon was roused by a light tapping on his hotel room door. It was so inconspicuous that he wasn't sure if was someone knocking or one of the many little rodent friends who frequented the hollow spaces behind the walls in the old hotel.

He got out of bed and made it to the door just in time to see a manila envelope slide under it. He peeked through the peephole but saw no one. He placed an ear to the door but heard no footsteps outside. He opened the door a crack. Just enough to see out but not unlinking the night chain. That only gave him a one way view of the hall but still no one. He closed the door and slid open the envelope. Inside was about fifty or sixty pages of Robinson's banking and corresponding documentation of his skimming from the military shipments under his command. Rick had come through.

Before heading to work Simon stopped in at his friendly desk attendant and begged another access to the office and this time the printer. He made three copies of the documents Rick had delivered. He put the originals in the envelope and in big bold letters marked Bradock on the front. This one he left at the bar where morning shift was just starting a pot of coffee. They assured him that they would get it to him. The other two he mailed from the front desk. One to his home address in Detroit and one himself. The last was another decoy. He hoped they would find it and think that that was the last of his sad attempts to avert the program.

He then headed to the elevator and down to the office to see what the day would bring.

No one was waiting for him today but the place was hopping. Even the lowly cubical rats were bent over their dividers like mice who had discovered that you didn't have to follow the maze you could actually climb over the wall if you wanted. Every one of them looked his way and gave the old thumbs up as he passed. He had no idea what was going on but he gave the sign right back. Didn't want them to think he was being kept in the dark.

He had just sat down when Nick launched himself through the door.

"So did you get the news?" he asked almost breathless.

"No, I just got in, what's going on?" Simon pretty much knew what was going on but he wanted Nick to give him the details.

"Some of our out facing satellites have the aliens on radar. According to the analysts it looks like they have slowed their speed but if they continue at their present rate and trajectory they should be in our atmosphere heading for somewhere in Nevada around noon tomorrow." Nick was pretty excited. Even though all his hard work would be for naught it still would be cool to see their baby in action.

"So what's the plan?" Simon asked.

That was Rick's que to slip in the door. He didn't say a word he just dropped an eight by ten sheet on Simon's desk and hurried away.

Both Nick and Simon hunched over the document.

The janitor knows the timing, a voice has told him were to

be to pick up his date. He also knows which lights to turn off and which ones to turn on.

Nick and Simon looked at each other. This could only mean that Wayne had figured out how to get Kim out and with Simpsons help she would be freed. Simpson was going to give Wayne the break he needed to escape as well.

Simon gave an audible sigh of relief. Nick put his hand on Simons shoulder. Now they would just have to play the game out and see what happened.

Simon ran the paper through the shredder then opened it up and took the lengths of paper to the washroom and flushed them down two separate stalls.

When he returned Robinson was sitting at his desk a big shit eating grin on his face.

"We're on." He said.

"What's that mean?" Simon countered.

"It means we're a day away from watching your invention take out a true to God threat to the American People. Judgment day son." He said it like he gave a shit.

Robinson got up and gave the office back to Simon. He turned just as he was at the door.

"Oh, just so you know, we put the pathogen back into your little mix so you don't have to worry about it working or not.

You and Nick are with me tomorrow. We're off to Nevada first thing so don't be late and don't get any ideas about taking off and trying to get your little girlfriend out of the shit show either."

Simon could hear him laughing as he walked down the corridor to the inner offices. He though if things worked out that dick will be wondering what the fuck happened. Not only to the great defense system that they had developed under his watchful eye but to all his petty larceny and the legacy of deceit that his father had handed down to him. Oh yea, tomorrow was going to be a judgment day but not the one that Robinson had hoped for.

The rest of the day Simon watched from his glass cage as the complex scurried in unctuous haste to ready all materials needed for launch or for transport to various parts of the world. They didn't know if the threat would be singular or if that singularity housed drones that could target other countries in the world. They thought the target would be America but they needed the rest of the wells strung out around the globe to be ready and on alert just in case.

His phone rang just before the end of the day. It was Robinson.

"Don't get lost and be back her at 0530 hours and don't be late."

It was all Simon could do to keep from charging down to Robinson office and beating the arrogant prick senseless. He had kept his composure for this long what was another twenty four hours. After that maybe he would loosen up some of Robinson's teeth.

The bar at the hotel looked too inviting to pass up. Simon needed a bourbon to calm his nerves otherwise he would never get to sleep.

The stool felt familiar and before long he had struck up a conversation with the bartender over his third drink. Mostly dry shit about how was work, what about the weather and when would the Redskins make the playoffs again. Three was enough for Simon. He could feel his eyelids starting to get heavy. He hadn't done much through the day but he had expended a lot of nervous energy just thinking about how all this would end. As he got up to leave his bartender friend said.

"Hey, before you go, the day crew said to tell you that Bradock dropped in for a quick one at lunch and got the package. He also said to tell you everything added up. If you know what that means."

Oh, he knew what that meant. Robinson was in for a double whammy. He wouldn't be late for tomorrow. In fact he could hardly wait.

A LONG DAY'S JOUNEY

Simon met Nick at the elevator in the hotel. Their brief discussion on the decent stopped abruptly as the doors opened and Robinson was standing there with two of the military police assigned to the project.

"Morning boys." Robinson was way too cheery. "I brought a couple of my friends along today to make sure you two didn't go missing in all the excitement."

"Fuck you." Simon said in his head. He wouldn't give the asshole the satisfaction of getting under his skin. As they made their way through the offices then back past the labs into the halls that led to the garage they picked up a person or two along the way. These were some of the original techs from their first successful launch. Computer analysts, atmospheric experts and satellite technicians.

"Where we heading" Simon asked, knowing exactly where they were going.

"It's E day" Robinson said with a smirk.

"What the hell is E day?" Nick spat back.

"The day we kill some aliens." Robinson turned to Nick. Nick didn't back down.

"Shouldn't that be A day then since the word Alien starts

with that letter?" Nicks response was met with a very imperceptible pause but it was long enough that everyone knew Robinson was an idiot.

"I can call it whatever the fuck I want to call it since I own this project." Robinson turned on his heel and stepped out of a steel plated door into the underground parking lot.

"Maybe if it was A day it would make more sense." Nick whispered. "Then the A could stand for A Hole and we all know who that is."

Simon liked that one but his attention was distracted by the space they had been led into and the number of black SUV's that lined the parking stalls. Robinson waved them toward one and climbed in the front seat.

"Where too?" the driver asked.

"Airport." That was the last word out of Robinson until they were all settled in to the company jet and speeding toward the Nevada firing range. "Ladies and Gentlemen." Robinson began. "This is it. We have confirmed satellite and radar positioning of an alien aircraft closing on our atmosphere. It's about three hundred thousand miles away, just this side of the moon. We should be able to get a better handle on the size of the craft or crafts in the next four hours.

We are currently on our way to our control center in Nevada. Once on site we will prep and prepare all Thunder

Wells from Metford Oregon to Houston Texas. We're pretty sure that's the area they will target."

How could you know that, Simon thought. I'll tell you how, you knew all along that the message in the wow signal wasn't a declaration of war, it was a rescue mission.

"Till then, keep it zipped and focus on the job at hand."

The two hour plane ride was accomplished in relative silence from the other scientists and tech's. Simon and Nick passed the time talking about how they were going to accomplish the mission, save the day and get out of the bunker in Nevada in one piece. They wondered at the obvious absence of Rick. Was he able to make the physical changes that would allow him to get to Roswell and aid in whatever was going to happen there?

At a point a few minutes before they began their decent Robinson walked passed and leaned in. "If you two love birds are wondering where you cohort Rick is, we made sure he wasn't making the trip."

"What do you mean by that?" Simon asked.

"Let's just say we were on to him and your little conspiracy group as soon as we found out you two detectives found our little underground secret. You two are so predictable. Listen to me, you guys are going to put this plan into action, you're going to make sure the shells reach their trajectory and deploy their payload and you're not going to try any more of your lame attempts to sabotage the program. Do that and when this is all over I might even put a good word in for your when we arrest you and whoever else you have helping you. Likely that dumb ass janitor out at the airport am I right?"

The fact that Robinson had some idea that the janitor Simpson was working with them was disturbing to say the least. The other comment made by Robinson that he had taken care of Rick in some way was also disconcerting. That left only Bradock. Their ace in the hole. Simon hadn't even let Nick in on the government agent he had met at the hotel bar. Why he had not confided in him he did not know but he thought now that their other compatriots had been found out it was probably a good thing he had kept the info to himself.

"Don't look so heartbroken. You two just don't get it do you. It's how the world goes around. We create the need and then supply the goods and take a commission for the effort. If it wasn't for that ship buried under the ground out in Roswell we would be using an abacas and calling it a computer. Almost all technological advances in the last fifty years are a direct result of reverse engineering stuff we pulled out of that space craft. If we can bring down this new threat we'll get another fifty years of advancement out of this one too. So finish your jobs and suck it up."

Robinson had used the word stuff in the middle of his

tirade so Simon knew that he didn't know square one about what he was talking about. He was obviously spouting some rhetoric overhead while in the company of someone with a greater understanding of technology than he.

Simon had had as much as he could stand of Robinsons moronic ramblings.

"So if that is true then who are Steve Jobs and Steve Wozniak?"

"Whoever they are they are probably working for us." Robinson turned and walked away.

Simon just looked open mouthed at Nick. "What a fucking lunatic." He mouthed to Nick.

The plane touched down at Hawthorne Municipal Airport, Nevada. The twenty five mile ride in the back of the old Ford Bronco had been made in silence. Now they were inside the bunker where many years before Simon had started his campaign to launch something into space from an earth bound well and recently proved that his ideas about using atomic charges to propel objects skyward at velocity was viable.

His quick glance at the surroundings and the people present matched pretty much with their last test firing of the well. The only one missing was Kim and as his thoughts went to her he wondered if by any chance in hell Simpson could pull off some kind of miracle and get her out of that underground cell and out of harm's way before everything went sideways. Kim was one thing. How they were going to manage the situation here was another.

"Ok boys, get to work" Robinson snapped.

As they walked toward the command consoles both Nick and Simon knew that Robinson had reintroduced the pathogen back into the mix, just as they had hoped he would. It totally took suspicion off of the fact that at altitude the virus would become inert. What bothered Simon was the second part of the plan. The launching of atomic weapons to blow the aliens out of the sky. It had always been a part of it but they had hoped that once the original virus had taken effect that they wouldn't have needed the second part. Now they knew that Robinson wouldn't be happy until he launched a couple of nukes as well.

As they traveled the length of each monitoring station Simon recognized someone. It was the electrician who had been on site when they set up the magneto to do the test launch. When their eyes met the guy put up a hand in greeting. Simon nodded back. At least one friendly face, he thought.

All the preparation looked like it was ready to go. They were getting a pretty good look at the size of the incoming craft from the satellite imagery. It was huge but they couldn't tell if it was a single ship or a number of smaller vessels in tight formation. Either way they were big.

"How long before they're in range?" Simon asked one of the techs manning the satellite feeds from high earth orbit. These satellites were flying at over 22,300 miles. That distance would cause about a 300 millisecond delay but still fast enough to be able to real time monitor the advance of the alien ship.

"Looks like maybe another hour or so. Then they should be within our framework for launch. We need about a sixty minute window to launch the virus projectiles and give the pathogen enough time to populate the space. That will also depend on the speed of the solar winds to disperse the payload."

"How many wells do we have on standby?" Nick wanted to know.

"One hundred and fifty from here to New Mexico. That was the launch line we were given by command."

That made sense. The Brass knew exactly where the returning ship or ships would head. Nevada was far enough away from ground zero to keep them safe and close enough if they needed to get to ground quickly they could do so.

SAVING GRACE

Rick had spent the last couple of days very uncomfortably re-aligning his skull and jaw bones to take on a more feminine look. The fourteen bones that make up his facial construction had been the worst. He would use the molecules of his hybrid skeletal structure to thin his nasal passages. Then he would look in the mirror to see if he had generated the correct effect. Once satisfied with that he moved on to cheek bones and so on until he had what he thought was a very feminine version of himself and once he got the brunette wig properly in place there was no way you could tell it was Rick. He looked like a very pretty twenty eight year old woman. Maybe a bit tall but he had had a harder time with his spinal configuration so he decided just to wear low cut shoes and slouch a little.

He had left his apartment in Washington and was now registered as Amanda Prentice at a little motel in Dexter, a small town just outside of Roswell. He had been in touch with Wayne since the second he got there and a plan was in place to get Kim out and Rick in. Rick had decided that his destiny lay with his father. What a crazy adventure that would be. The government labs had made him into something other than human so why not take advantage of that. Why not go exploring in the stars. It was every boys dream to fly to another world and it had always been Ricks, ever since Star

Trek hit the air in the sixties. That was long before he had realized he was anything other than a real human kid.

Wayne had contacted him telepathically and they had worked out a plan with Simpson the janitor Simon had talked about back at the lab.

Simpson had discovered where the breaker switch was for the power that fed the magnets holding Wayne's ship in place. He was on board. His job was to get Kim out of harm's way and out of the airport grounds to a safe place before the shit hit the fan. They would let him know the timing. Since they didn't have to phone to give him the heads up they could plot it down to the second.

Rick would subdue the guards that were usually somewhere between hangars. He had a gun that he had bought in town at a hardware store and some industrial zip ties. He was confident he would not have to use the gun. There had always been a group of two who guarded the entrance to the subterranean ship. Since Simon and Nick had found their way below the field a third had been added. These men rotated a day and night shift for one year before being replaced. The job was boring so they found ways to pass the time and had become complacent over time. It was the same with the very new rotation and it would be no different with the three who held the position now. They weren't heroes. They would willingly allow themselves to be tethered rather than the alternative which was a very long ride in an alien space ship.

It would be fairly simple. They picked a different office to lounge in every other day. Nothing much ever happened on their watch. They only thing they had missed in fifty years was Nick and Simons little adventure underground.

That one had got by them but still they hadn't been overly reprimanded for the failure so they were just as content to sit in one of the offices and sip coffee laced with whisky and listen to the radio till they fell asleep.

Once Kim was out of the hole and Rick had made his way in Simpson would turn off the power to the magnets. Wayne and Rick would give them enough time to get out of the way and then they would be off.

For more than fifty years Wayne had lived on in his dungeon. Long after his two traveling companions had succumb to the dark and the lack of proper medical treatment for what on their world would have been minor ailments but here, once their own medical supplies were gone, could not be treated and they eventually died of their diseases.

The teams of interrogators had finally given up after they exhausted every form of mental and physical torture they could come up with. All they wanted, they said, was to know how the propulsion system worked and though Wayne knew exactly how it worked and could have built an exact replica given the materials but he was never going to tell them that. He knew that their promises of letting him go if he divulged the secrets were thinly veiled lies. The funny part was that they had no idea that because of his carbon based physical structure any of the physical torture they attempted to use had absolutely no effect. Hell he couldn't feel a thing. Same with the psychobabble and the mental tricks. He could hear their thoughts. He knew what was coming before they did. Even the drugs they had pumped into him had no effect. His cellular structure was immune to anything from this world that was hallucinogenic or toxic.

All in all it had been a long and tedious time. He would really like to see the sun again. He would remember his fallen crew but now he had allies and this would be his only chance to go.

FINAL COUNT DOWN

All one hundred and fifty of the wells had been loaded and checked. They were ten minutes from launch and Simon was nervously going over everything in his head.

Had Rick really been stopped or worse? Did Simpson have a plan if so? Did Bradock have a plan and if so would he be able to convince anyone that this was really happening? How were he and Nick going to get out of this in one piece?

All these questions would have to wait. The rest of the world had been put on standby as the Nevada control center started countdown to launch. Simon hoped that every one of the wells would blow up on ignition but he knew they had thought through every scenario in development and that just wasn't going to happen.

The usual suspects were huddled together. Heads bowed, whispering to each other each conspirator with his agenda. Now that they knew Robinson was not the brains but the muscle it wouldn't be too long before the real boss show his colors. As soon as they found out the virus was not going to work one of the other four would have to start making decisions and Simon was interested to see who that might be. The two security guard's Robinson had assigned to them were never more than a few feet away. They clung to them like a mohair sweater. Where the hell would he go? The place was a dungeon. The only way out was the heavily guarded steel door that would not open without the help of hydraulics and a key pad.

Simon put these thoughts aside as he watched the digital clock tick down. Fifteen minutes left and it couldn't be too soon for him. There was nothing else he or Nick could do but wait and see.

There was very little chatter in the control center. The hushed whispers of the brass were mostly drowned out with updates on barrel and projectile readiness. The time would not be physically counted down until the last minute.

Nick shuffled over and stood next to Simon at one of the control panels that monitored the flight path of the projectile.

"Hey, do you think that they really did something to Rick or was that just Robinson bullshitting us to try and scare us?" Nick didn't sound scared more concerned about Rick. It was after all he who had got Rick involved in the plot to sabotage the project and even though it had turned out that Rick was actually the project he still didn't want to have been the cause of any harm that might have come to him.

"I have a funny feeling that Robinson is full of shit in many ways. He may have inherited this whole scam from his father but I don't think he's got half the brain his old man had.

Otherwise he wouldn't be scrambling to make this work right now. I know one thing. He might be desperate enough to not let us get out of this with our skin intact." Simon had thought that Robinson was a desperate man and would do almost anything to keep his status quo.

"I was thinking the same thing." Nick replied "and I can tell you that I won't be going down without a fight. The first chance I get after the wells go off I'll be making a move to get a gun."

"Let's see what happens after the launch. Keep separated so there are two different targets. I'll stay close to the control frame and you see if you can get up back near the brass." That will make it harder for them to control both of us."

"Ok, but if I see any hinky shit from Robinson, I'm moving." Nick sounded tough. Simon just hoped for a miracle.

The satellite imagery showed the alien craft on the monitors. Not in detail but that didn't matter. One of the analysts sitting near Simon hit the nail on the head. "That thing is fucking gigantic." Simon would have to agree. He had seen satellite imagery of returning space craft and this was nothing even in the same ball park. In fact it was more like about ten ball parks put together.

The ship had come to a halt pretty much where the team had hoped. Just inside the outside the first layer of the earth's atmosphere.

If the original plan had still been in play it would have been the perfect scenario for their little floating virus to do its dirty work.

The control center was on pins and needles. Most of the team had never really believed that there would be alien invaders. They thought it was just another government three hundred dollar hammer. Must have been quite the shock to actually see the thing just sitting there staring down at the cameras. Matter of fact since the imagery had come through there had been a huge hike in the bathroom breaks.

The clock was ticking down. The com controller started the final ten seconds. Simon realized he was sweating. Too bad Kim wasn't going to see this go off first hand.

The count hit zero and Simon just reached out and nonchalantly hit the firing button. No more effort than starting the car or lighting a cigarette.

The monitors focused on the well took only a second before the screen was whited out as the projectile left the hole followed by a huge flash of gas and fire. The whomp that followed was exactly like the test firing but still shook the hideout and sent those standing looking for a hand hold.

The telescope telemetry had been dialed in since they had last been on site so they picked up the speeding projectiles almost instantaneously. In his excitement Simon's immediate concerns of the day were swept away as a decades old idea came to fruition. He was surprised at how much emotion welled up in him as the tiny projectile headed for space carrying its useless payload but launching a dream he had had since childhood. It was as exhilarating as he had hoped it would be.

A cheer went up from the room as the bullet traveled out past the first level of atmosphere. Nicks hand on his shoulder made Simon turn to shake his paw.

"Well, it worked." Nick had a big smile on." "Probably couldn't have gone much smoother."

"Now let's hope all our other plans fall into place." Nick replied. "We are running blind here so I think we are going to need a certain amount of luck."

"Luck or not. I'm kicking the crap out of Robinson when this is all over." Simon looked into Nicks face and saw no fear just determination.

Both men turned to watch the progression of the cylinder and the tracking of the other one hundred and forty nine wells that had detonated at the same time. It would not take long for them all to reach their targeted altitude. The payload would disperse just as it did in the trials the only difference would be that no one was going to get sick and die. Taking the sterile virus out of the mix to let Robinson put it back in had been a stroke of genius. He probably thought he single handedly kept them from sabotaging the program. It was all Simon could do not to gloat.

Nick had moved back to the back of the control room as planned. They were still half an hour out from the projectiles reaching critical altitude where the canister would detonate and disperse the nanites.

"Alright listen up." The loud barking commands turned every head in the room. Robinson had come down from the observation area and was standing just behind the computer monitors and control panels. "I want the war heads placed in the wells. Notify all other facilities that just launched and have them arm the wells with the nukes."

"What the fuck are you doing? Simon's voice was more than a little raised. "You can't arm those. That was a secondary precautionary measure only to be implemented if the virus didn't work."

"You're not making that call. I am. It's a military decision and I'm the military. I'm not going to wait and see. It could be too late by then so let's get on those calls and get the other wells armed." The entire place was mesmerized. They just stared. "Right fucking now." Robinson screamed the order. He looked straight at Simon for a second and then smiled like he had just shit in his pants before walking back to the observation deck.

Simon's anger was at its limit. With balled fists he turned in pursuit of the smug bastard. He didn't give a shit what happened now. He was going to break someone's nose.

His first step was swiftly halted as a strong hand grabbed his lab coat sleeve and pull him to a stop. Robinson had his back turned to the floor so he didn't see the look on Simon's face nor the man who had stopped him in his tracks.

He turned on his assailant with as much hate for whoever it was as he had for Robinson. He had assumed it was going to be one of the Military Police that had accompanied them to the bunker. The face of the electrician caught him off guard.

"I got this he said."

"What Simon retorted?"

"Trust me, we've been onto Robinson since you gave Bradock the files on him and the rest of this craziness. Stay calm and don't start anything. Just do what you're supposed to do and we'll take care of the rest."

With that the man turned and went back to his place beside the maintenance panel that housed the breakers and heat and air control systems for the bunker.

What the fuck is going on now? Simon thought. This could not get any more confusing if it had too. How did this guy know about Bradock? Jesus, was everything a conspiracy?

Nick had noticed the incident with the electrician and came over to find out what was going on. "What just happened there?" he asked.

"Not too sure but I was going to push Robinsons nose into his skull when the electrician grabbed me and told me to keep calm he had it under control. He also mentioned a guy I gave some inside information too. I met a guy at the bar in the Mayflower" I didn't tell you because I wasn't sure he could do anything for us.

"How the hell…."

"I know, its crazy right? I have a feeling we should do as he says. Somethings going on here and we don't have control of it."

"I hear ya, and I'm cool with letting things play out but I'm still going to get a few licks into that prick before we're done." Simon thought Nick would too.

As he turned back to watch the minions making the wells ready for the nukes he stole a glance in the direction of the electrician. No response, not even a nod.

Simon just turned back to the monitors and stared.

They were minutes away from the nanite dispersal and he wanted to at least see that work before the shit hit the fan.

ISLAND IN THE SKY

Since Simon and Nick had found their way into the cavern beneath the Airport there had been an extra guard assigned to the normal two man patrol. Simpson was in the process of relaying this information to Rick while still recovering from the shock of Rick showing up as a woman.

"Well two or three really won't make much of a difference." Rick told him. "Because of my carbon structure they really can't hurt me and it would take more than three to overpower me. I don't think they are going to suspect a lost woman looking for directions to pull a gun and tie them up, do you?"

Simpson had to agree with that but he was going to make sure that he was in close proximity to the action just in case. He had checked out the hangar they were in tonight by scanning the drag strip out buildings with his night vision field glasses.

He kept a pair of the glasses to save himself some time when on night shift. The glasses saved him from having to tour the grounds in the golf cart.

He could see that the lights were on in the last hangar to the south. He knew these buildings inside and out so he had filled Rick in on exactly where the office was in relation to the front door. Rick would have to find a way to get from the front door to the office without tipping his hand. Even though Rick looked like a woman the guards would still be a bit suspicious of someone all the way out there in the night.

He would have to get them all in the room at the same time to be able to force them to comply.

Rick pulled the gun out that he had bought in Dexter. It was a Lugar replica .22 caliber hand gun but it looked a lot bigger than it was. It would do the job. It fooled Simpson if nothing else.

"Think you're going to have to use that?" he asked.

"I hope not but I will if they try to shoot me. Let's get going"

It was dusk. Rick had driven in on Will Rodgers Road and Simpson now gave him the directions on how to follow it to the drag strip.

Simpson would follow in the golf cart coming around to the strip from the airport side. He would wait and see if all went well with Rick's ruse. If he got the signal he would proceed to the building where Simon and Nick and ultimately Kim had the experience with the humming floor. This was where he had discovered the four huge breakers that would turn of the generators to the magnets holding Wayne captive.

Simpson had discovered the breakers completely by

accident. Sure, he was looking for them. After he had the conversation with Simon and knew that the young lady was being held captive he felt that it was time he did something. He could no longer keep quiet about what was going on. How could he live with himself if something happened to that girl? He had climbed up into the rafters of the building to clean out some birds' nests that had gone from two to about ten. How they got in he could not figure out but it was time to take them down. Once up on the ladder he noticed that what he had assumed was an old air-conditioning unit was in fact just a fake housing that looked even more fake at close range. He unscrewed the top and there they were, four very large breakers build into the rafters. He was almost tempted to turn them off then and there but at the time he still hoped that he would make it to retirement without having to get involved.

Now he sat quietly watching as Rick passed by in his rental car on his way down the line of buildings. He would know soon enough if they would be successful.

Rick saw Simpson parked on the north side of one of the buildings as he pulled into the drag strip off Will Rodgers and headed for the last of the structures that serviced it. As he parked in front he cleared his throat and tried the voice he would use to fool the guards.

They must have head the car as he had barely gotten out when the door to the building opened and two guards cautiously poked their heads out guns pointed.

Rick let out a little "Oh." And put his hands up. Enough to cover his mouth but not too high as he didn't want them to see the gun holstered under his arm.

"I'm sorry he said." he kept his voice low so not to give away his true nature. "I'm lost and I saw your light on. I thought you could help me or maybe had a phone.

"This is a restricted area." One of the men barked.

"I didn't know." Rick did his best to sound scared. "It got dark and I was just driving around in circles." If you could I just need to call my mother to let her know I'm ok and if you could give me directions, please. I have some money I can pay for the phone call."

Just as he spoke Rick made to reach in the purse he was carrying as part of his disguise. As he fumbled with the lock he dropped the purse spilling its contents on the ground at his feet.

"I'm so sorry." he gasped. "I'm just a bit flustered."

"Ok, look lady, this is a restricted area but if you're quick you can use the phone in the office." One of the guards said as he bent to help Rick pick up the purses contents.

Rick followed the two back into the building. A real team would have had one guard in front and one behind him if they knew what they were doing he thought. These two obviously didn't think he was any kind of threat. Now if the third one was also in the office he could zip them up in a neat little bow.

The third guard was pretty much asleep on a dirty leather couch pushed against the side wall of the office. The other two just walked in ahead of Rick so when they turned around and saw the gun in his hand one of them let out a little laugh.

Rick promptly shot him in the leg.

His screams woke up the one on the couch while the one left standing started to talk.

"Now just a minute miss. I don't know what you're up to here but their ain't no money or anything of value. We just look after the buildings and keep the kids off the drag strip at night."

"Sure you do." Rick replied. He no longer needed to disguise his voice. "Just get on your hands and knees or I'll give you a taste of what your buddy just got."

It didn't take a second request. Rick had all three zip tied and gaged with a couple of wash cloths he had brought from the hotel before Simpson came crashing into the building.

"Hey, I heard the gun go off and came as fast as I could. You ok?"

Rick was good. He just gave Simpson a quick nod and pointed to the door.

"Just got a head note from Wayne. Do you know what he's talking about? Some elevator in the trailer?"

The only trailer that Simpson could think of was the one that was behind the building where he had discovered the breakers.

"I think so. What's up?

"Wayne says you got to turn off the generators and I need to go to the trailer to get down to the ship."

"What about the girl?" Simpson asked.

"He's going to send her up before I go down. Then you two gotta get the hell out of here as fast as you can. Take the rental I left back at the other building and go north. Just make sure you're not within a couple of miles of this place in about ten minutes."

Simpson led him to the back of the building where the trailer was and headed in to turn off the breakers. The vibration in the floor still gave him a buzz after all this time. He wouldn't be sad to not feel that ever again.

Rick pulled open the door to the trailer where Simon and Nick had started their adventure into the depths of an alien world. He no sooner entered when he heard a slam from one of the doors about half way down from the entrance. When he pulled it open he found a dazed and confused Kim staring at him like he was her long lost brother.

Kim just threw her arms around him and said, "Wayne says there's a catch for the elevator locked into the side of the vanity."

Rick ran his hands down both sides of the sink and quickly found what he was looking for. "You better get out of here." He said. "Simpson is in the building right outside and knows what to do. Thanks, tell Simon and Nick good luck."

Kim wasted no time in exiting the trailer. She heard the slam of the elevator as it made its way down to the alien air craft for the last time. She pulled open the door to the building where not so long ago she had been taken prisoner. Simpson was just on the other side of the door. He grabbed her hand and told her to run. She held on and followed his lead back to the rental left at the last building in line.

The keys were in the ignition and Simpson didn't even take time to see if the guards had escaped or not. He just punched the gas and headed North on Will Rogers road as fast as the shitty little four cylinder would go.

Simpson had turned onto 255 off of Will Rogers. Neither one had said a word since entering the car. Kim looked frazzled but Rick had told Simpson to get the hell away from the area as fast as he could and that was exactly what he was doing.

Kim sat slouched in the corner of the seat her head resting

on the window. Her hair was a bit bedraggled but other than that she didn't seem any less for the wear.

The rumbling started just as they were about to get onto Hobson Road and Highway 285. Simpson hadn't looked back he was just hell bent on getting them as far away as they could get.

As they made the turn on to Hobson Road a huge boom shook the ground. The rumbling was now coming as tremors beneath the wheels of the vehicle and Simpson had to pull off in a dirt siding to keep the car from going in the ditch.

It was like an earthquake. The car was shaking so violently that Kim and Simon had to get out. From their vantage point the lights that lit up the runways at the airport gave them a clear view of the field next to the drag strip. What they saw would remain with them for the rest of their lives.

As they gazed in the direction that the horrendous sounds were coming from a gigantic pile of earth began to rise out of the ground. Before their eyes a massive floating island began to take shape. As it gained altitude a couple of hundred feet of rock, earth and scrub brush began to slide from the black hull. Its impact sent a shock wave that took windows out all around the area.

The craft was gigantic in its blackness. What had felt like a couple of playing fields underground was in fact now a two kilometer wide flying space ship. It rose slowly from its grave as if sighing in relief at the end of its long internment. Suddenly there was a ripple in the air, a shock wave of such intensity that the two onlookers could hear their hair singeing as the ozone burned around them before it knocked them up against the car. Then without a single sound the hovering black island went straight up out of sight so fast it was like a magic trick.

The following silence was deafening as the alien aircraft sucked air and oxygen alike along with it in its extraordinary exodus. Not a sound from traffic or planes arriving or going from the airport. No creatures of the night made little burrowing noises as they scurried away from the earthquake. It was as if in a vacuum the world had seen its future.

Simpson looked at Kim his mouth just slightly less agape than hers.

"Holy shit." He exclaimed. "Did you see that?

Kim could only look away and stare back at the dark sky of the night. The stars were out but she wasn't looking at them. She was still trying to peer into the void to try and catch one last glimpse of what even seconds later felt like a hallucination.

It was a full twenty minutes before either of them spoke. Lost in their own thoughts they just lent against the car and stared at the sky. For anyone passing by they might have thought the two were star gazers stopped outside the city where the street lamps wouldn't impair their view of the night sky.

Finally Simpson broke the silence. "I guess I had better get you somewhere a little safer than here right now. I would take you to my place but there will probably be someone coming looking for me. Rick left the key to the motel he was staying at on the front seat. I know the place. No one would likely know the difference if it was you or Rick who was occupying the room for the next couple of days."

Kim heard the words come floating back into her consciousness like she was waking from a dream. She only caught the last part of what Simpson had been saying. Something about using the room Rick had rented to hide out until what?

"I'm not really sure how long you would be able to stay there. Rick didn't say how long he rented it for and I don't really know how you're going to get in touch with your friends to let them know that you're safe and where you are."

Kim couldn't think of any other option right at that moment. They had just witnessed one of the most incredible events in the history of mankind so at this point the hotel would have to do.

"Ok then, let's go and you can fill me in on what's been happening on the way."

NUKES AWAY

The projectiles had reached critical altitude and the small detonators had opened the war heads to release the nanites to the wind. Only Nick and Simon were privy to the fact that the now sterile pathogen was just that and they were really only interested in seeing if the concept of releasing these microscopic mechanics into the solar winds was a viable defense system for future reference.

Imagery was coming in from the other one hundred and fifty wells and it appeared that all of the projectiles but one had delivered their payload. One misfire would not break the program. These nanites had not been affected with any kind of phosphorus or luminescence so there was no way of seeing the little buggers or telling if they had disbursed in the way that Simon had projected but he felt great pride in the fact that all the mechanics of the program worked perfectly and that he and Nick had no part in the death of any sentient being.

He had been so enamored with watching the satellites and listening to the updated data coming in from the other wells that he hadn't noticed Nick.

"Somethings up. Nick whispered.

Simon looked at Nick and then slowly pursued the rest of the bunker.

"Robinson has been off in the corner on his phone and even though he's talking under his breath he looks really upset. I think the shit is about to hit the fan."

Simon tracked down Robinson in behind the other members of the board none of whom were taking much notice of him.

Robinson abruptly ended his conversation and hurried to the front of the control center.

"Attention everyone. I have just had a conversation with our head of army intelligence and I have been informed that they have broken incoming alien code and are now positive that they are our enemy. They are preparing to launch a host of God knows what at us and we have gone to Defcon 1."

"That's bullshit." Simon yelled. "You haven't even given the nanites the opportunity to spread or work. How do they know that attack is eminent?'

"That is not for me to question. I do know that we have been given the green light to launch the ballistics in the wells. Please inform the other locations that they need to lock and load ASAP. They have five minutes to launch."

"You can't do this." Simon still couldn't believe what he was hearing. Those wells have never been tested with the real atomic warheads. You don't know if they'll fly or if they will just create a hundred and fifty giant holes from Nevada to New

Mexico."

"This is what's going to happen. I am now in control of this facility. If you don't want to be handcuffed and locked away for the duration you will do as I say and keep your mouth shut. If I see you or your sidekick there doing anything suspect I have the right to shoot you and I will. So sit down and shut the fuck up."

Neither Nick nor Simon sat down but they backed away just enough to be out of Robinson's line of site.

"What do you think we should do now?" Nick said under his breath.

"I thought that Robinsons boss was one of the other four members of the brass. I see now that that person is keeping themselves at arms distance and letting Robinson take the fall if anything goes sideways.

"We should start trying to figure out a way to sabotage this whole place if we can. There is something else going on here. I wonder if Rick and Simpson pulled of the great escape. Now Robinson is covering his ass by trying to blow that ship up to prove there was a clear and eminent threat. That would forward his funding for all the new arms and development he would need for the rest of his life. One other thing. A while ago I made a move to re-arrange Robinson's nose and our trusty electrician there stopped me."

"What do you mean?" Nick asked.

"Well, he grabbed my shirt and held me back and sort of said, *he had this* in a real conspiratorial way, if you know what I mean?"

"I'm assuming by 'this' he meant the situation here in control?" Nick sounded confused.

"That's how I took it."

He basically knows about Robinson and that I gave critical documents regarding Robinson and the mission of this project to this guy Bradock that I met at the Mayflower.

Both men looked over at the man in question and were both greeted with a nod. *What the hell was his game?* Simon thought. Was he for or against what was going on? Either way they would have to try and stop Robinson somehow.

"How come you never told me about this Bradock guy?" Nick asked.

"Sorry, it's a long story and I wasn't sure if he could help or if it would just be too late so I didn't want to get your hopes up."

"Well if this guy is saying he talked to this Bra dock guy maybe he did find a way to do something." Nick sounded hopeful.

Both men turned back to the monitor only to be met by the

two military police that had escorted them from the lab that morning.

"Gentlemen, you will please come with us." They each took an arm and escorted Simon and Nick to the observation level of the bunker. Once ensconced far enough away that it would be virtually impossible for either of them to make a play to stop Robinson they were sat in a couple of chairs with their monitors standing right beside them. They were told to put their hands behind their backs and Simon could hear the rattling of the hand cuffs as his left wrist was firmly encircled by the metal band. As the officer bent to his second hand he leaned in close enough so only Simon could hear. "Don't move. We are not with Robinson. Bradock got word to his superiors and we are just giving him enough rope to hang himself. The weapons will never fire so just sit here and enjoy the show.

"Was anything ever above board? Was anything the government did ever just what it was instead of a mystery wrapped in a puzzle only solvable with another puzzle?"

Nick had head the hushed words as well and was looking as dazed as Simon. He was just about to mouth something when Robinson called to the controllers for an update on the loading of the other wells.

"All wells accounted for sir." The head controller

confirmed.

"Well then, we don't need any fancy countdown for this hit the fucking button." Robinson was so enwrapped in his role as Earth savior that he had just thrown all protocol out the window. When his command was met with blank stares he just yelled at the man with his hand on the firing pin.

"Launch the God damned things you idiot."

"I don't have the authority to do that sir." The controller said.

"Well who the fuck does?" Robinson was livid.

"The command can only be issued by the President or by someone carrying his briefcase." The controller looked white as a sheet. It was obvious he was in over his head and who could blame him. He didn't want to be the one responsible for any kind of an atomic launch let alone one that might end in inter planetary bloodshed. That thought alone in its insanity was enough to make him balk at the idea of sending a hundred and fifty atomic warheads into space.

"Well that would be me." Robinson proclaimed. "I have the permission of the president." He just crossed the space between himself and where the controller sat, flipped up the protective casing on the launch button and slammed his hand down on it.

There was a sharp intake of air as the entire control center sucked in their respective breaths. They were shocked. Everyone immediately switched focus to the big screens that monitored the well.

Where was the blast? There should have been an immediate response to the firing pin. No giant cloud of gas and no thunder clap followed by the moving of the earth that signaled the firing of the well.

"What happened?" Robinson screamed. "Did you fuck with it so it wouldn't work?" he asked the now frightened controller.

"No. I don't know what went wrong." The controller turned and looked back at Nick and Simon.

"Don't look at those two fuckups." Robinson yelled. He had his gun pulled and was pointing it at the controller who was now as white as a ghost and looked like he might just pass out at any second. "Make it work or else."

What happened next took everyone by surprise. The two military police who had subdued Simon and Nick had come up behind Robinson in what looked like a supportive position. No one was more surprised than Robinson when they took him by the arms kicked his legs out from under him and in the blink of an eye had him handcuffed and on the floor.

When Robinson realized what had happened the litany of curses mitigated only by the threats of discharge and finally what he was going to do to them when the pentagon found out about how he was being treated would have filled the pentagon.

When he finally ranted himself out the electrician stood over him and read him the riot act.

Hello, Sargent Robinson. I am special agent Williams. I report directly to the Commanding General of The United States Army Criminal Investigation Command. We have been watching your sorry ass for a long time. You are under arrest. I will not list the counts against you because I don't have all day but let's just say you will not be seeing the outside of prison for a very long time.

Someone started to applaud and the whole room joined in.

Simon and Nick would have followed suit but they were still tethered to the folding chairs. One of the military police looked in their direction and Nick hollered at him over the din to get the locks off.

It was special agent Williams who did the honors. "How did you know what Robinson was up too and why didn't the nukes fire? Simon wanted to know.

"It's a long story Simon. The short version is we have been watching Robinson and those in his circle of friends for some time. Long before this Thunder Well thing came up. We didn't really believe the whole alien thing right from the start and it wasn't until you gave the proof to Bradock, who is one of us by the way, that we saw the truth. We were as astonished as you likely where the first time Nick told you about it. Any way we were just waiting for Robinson to go too far. He has a lot of friends in high official places in the government and the military. Mostly handed down from his old man but still loyal to the kick back money he supplied them to look the other way. We needed him to get himself in so deep there would be no rescue from any quarter. Finding out that the alien plot was real was pretty crazy so we just let the whole game play out.

The real warheads never would have detonated. Even if they had of launched. They have to be armed. We had changed all the arming codes weeks ago. Sorry we couldn't step in with Kim. It would have given us away. I can tell you that she is safe and out of harm's way. We will send an escort tomorrow to bring her home. In the mean time we have the phone number of the motel she is staying at so you can call and see that she is good.

If you're wondering, your friend Rick and whoever was driving that space ship are gone. You left a hint that there might be something of interest to be seen at the Roswell airport if anyone was interested and you were right. It was more than interesting. It was the stuff movies are made out of.

That's it for now. We will take up more of your time on another day because we will need to fully debrief you and the rest of your team. I don't what parts of this are to be kept secret and what aren't but I will advise you to keep it all to yourself until we talk. We will take you and Nick back to Washington but please make yourselves available in the next few days to begin debriefing."

"Hey look at this." Someone yelled from one of the near space monitoring panels. "It looks like our new friends are retreating."

They huddled around the monitor and watched as the vast expanse of the alien invaders craft gained speed and headed back out to space.

"Looks like the snot bombs must have scared them off." He said.

"Yea, what do you know? It actually worked." Simon looked at Nick and just grinned. No sense in tell them anything different. They would have a hell of story for their grandkids. That is if they could ever tell them about the day they saved earth from alien invaders with nothing more than a couple of strategically dug wells and bombs full of mucus.

"So." Nick said. "Looks like Rick and Simpson pulled it off. Man I would have loved to have been there when that thing came flying out of the ground. I wonder if anyone got a picture of that?"

"I'm just relieved that Kim was able to get out."

"Let's get the hell out of here." Nick exclaimed. "I need a drink. Wait, scratch that. I need a bunch of drinks."

"I hear you loud and clear. Last one to the Mayflower is buying."

They both flew home on the same plane they had arrived in and were driven to the Mayflower. That night after a quick phone call to Kim's room in Dexter the two friends sat and recounted the last year. It had been insane. Both had achieved what they had set out to do. Simon proved his wells worked and Nick had invented a new way of deploying strategic materials at the molecular level.

It was many beers and many more tequilas before Simon staggered to his room and Nick was helped into a cab home.

ALL'S WELL

Simon's little street in Detroit was lit with a standard street light every so many feet. The yellow glow of the aging lenses and the large overhanging oak trees gave it the iconic look of an old Hollywood movie. There was even a 1967 Oldsmobile Toronado parked in one of the drives giving even more credence to the illusion.

Simons back deck was far enough from the harsh light of the street that you could see thousands of stars on a clear nigh. Occasionally a loud trucks passing on the highway miles away would disturb the cool early summer air but even that could not break the spell of the glittering menagerie above.

It had been three months of fairly intense interrogation before Kim, Nick and Simon were allowed to return to their homes. Nick and Simon to Detroit and Kim to New York. It was funny. Up until they were released from their debriefing Simon had never even asked Kim where her home was. He was surprised when she said New York City. He had somehow thought they would all end up back in Detroit together.

For the last three months in Washington the three friends had been sequestered. No contact with each other had been allowed. On their last day they had been gathered in a conference room and told that they were no longer needed and that they would be contacted if there was anything else that needed to be clarified. There contacts while sequestered had been Simons Mayflower contact, Bradock and the electrician from the Nevada control center, Williams.

"We wanted to bring you three together to thank you for doing everything you did to bring Robinson to us and to try and do the right thing in a difficult situation. We can tell you now that Robinson rolled on every single one of his contacts including those that had been farmed by his father. It will take yeas but none of them will got off the hook for what they have done." With that Williams and Bradock stood and shook their hands.

There is a car waiting to take you to the airport. Thanks again and good luck."

As they headed together to the airport Simon suggested that they stay in touch and get together soon. Kim had asked "when?" Simon had replied. "Call anytime and come for a tour of Detroit."

To his surprise that call came two weeks later. The phone ringing in the kitchen was weird. He could count on both hands and part of a foot the number of calls he had received at home in the last five years.

The voice on the other end of the line was a bit of a surprise as well. "Hey Simon, its Kim. I was thinking I could take you up on that offer for a free Detroit tour." Simon was glad to hear her voice. "I didn't expect to hear from you so soon. I would have thought after all that happened you would want to take some time."

"Funny you mention that. Now that I'm home even New York feels a bit dull. You know, no conspiracies to mention, no aliens to be captive with or any hidden underground space ships to wander around in."

"Well I don't know if I can dig up any alien conspiracies here for you but we do have some nice restaurants and I do have some cold beer and tequila on hand so let me know when you're coming and I'll pick you up."

They had slept together the first night Kim was in town. That was a month ago and since then they had toured Detroit, done a little sailing on the great lakes, even taken in a baseball game. Nick had joined them on some of their travels but mostly they had just spent time together. Kim had told Simon that their age difference didn't matter to her. She was more interested in someone with intelligence and a good sense of humor than anything else. He was glad because he really enjoyed her company.

Now as they sat together on the deck they sipped their tequila and stared up at the stars knowing that someone was out there looking back. Both enjoying the night, both catching their breath and then laughing as they watched each falling star blaze and then peter out.

THE END

www.ingramcontent.com/pod-product-compliance
Lightning Source LLC
Chambersburg PA
CBHW071126200626
46817CB00018B/2230